Private Eye

The first adventure of Jason Streak

By

Joshua A. Rodriguez

Table of Contents

PREFACE...5

CHAPTER 1...7

CHAPTER 2...17

CHAPTER 3...39

CHAPTER 4...47

CHAPTER 5...57

CHAPTER 6...65

CHAPTER 7...73

CHAPTER 8...81

CHAPTER 9...91

CHAPTER 10..100

CHAPTER 11..110

CHAPTER 12..116

CHAPTER 13..122

PREFACE

As a child, I was always fascinated by the wonders of books. One genre that I enjoyed very much was mysteries. I enjoyed them so much that I began creating my own short stories. To this day I still have in my possession the notebook in which I wrote them. As my reading comprehension matured, so did my eagerness to continue reading. Looking back, I feel had I never picked up that first mystery novel then I may have not discovered the adventures of reading. I wrote this book with the expectation that I too could influence young readers and captivate them in the joys and benefits of reading. I first began writing this book in early 2009 and completed it after many years of constructing the perfect mystery novel. Most of my ideas from when I began writing were scrapped because it thought it was too dark for young adults. I made it my goal, to write a book that was suitable for all ages. I intend on making this book into a series.

CHAPTER 1

"Jason Streak strikes down crime once again. Read more about this heated tale on page nine," Jason read out loud for his partner to hear. "Page nine, they can't be serious," he said as he scrolled through the newspaper quickly. "Holy crap, we are on page nine, can you believe this Ryan?"

"I hear you, Jason. You know it's not the first time we have been featured in a newspaper." Ryan was looking out the window, enjoying the view. The sun was shining hard on the city; all the cars below were reflecting the sunlight. It made him feel like he was looking directly at the sun. But he didn't want to look away. The view was beautiful to him and well worth straining his eyes.

Jason turned around in his chair to look at him, "You're sightseeing again. I guess you really want to be the world's first blind detective."

"Don't worry; my health care will cover it."

"My eyes still hurt from last time. I was curious and decided to see what you were so fond of, man do I regret it."

"It takes very little effort to squint your eyes."

"If you need to squint to look, then I don't think it's worth it. What's so special about the view anyway, it's just a bunch of cars?"

"I like the way the city looks from up here. Besides, it's sunny today. The weather has been utter crap this past week."

"But it's the same view every day. I will admit it does change the way you see the city."

"Yeah, the city looks a lot more peaceful."

"The view is a bit overrated, just take a picture of it and put it on your desk. I still think it was a mistake to move our office here."

"Why? We have an office in the city now, and the rent is not that expensive."

"That's all true, but this office is also twenty stories up. What if the elevator breaks down, do you think our clients will climb all those stairs? If the elevator is not working, I'm not coming in. There's also almost no room in here."

"Jason, for the price we are paying we can't complain. Sometimes you have to cut some corners to get what you want."

"Please elaborate."

"Turn to page nine and you'll see what I mean."

Jason picked the newspaper back up and opened it, "What about page nine, they wrote about us. Unbelievable, I smash through two glass panes to catch the criminal and this is all I get? That case was at least page three worthy but we got stuck on page nine."

"At least we got the murderer, Jason. I'm just happy that he'll get what he deserves."

"You know my motto. We put them away, that's what we do."

"Jason, you know what I always say. Your motto sucks."

"Yeah, whatever, it will grow on you. By the way what time is it right now?"

"It's like three pm, why?"

"Shouldn't those painters be here by now? Soon we'll have clients barging through the door. We can't have this place looking this bad for long."

Their new office was some piece of work. Not only was it small, but it was also hard on the eyes. The condition of the walls was so bad, that Jason had to hire painters to paint them. The only furniture in the office was a couple of chairs, a desk and a couch that Ryan brought from his house. Their old office was bigger and better in every way possible. But, since their work didn't require much space or fancy rooms, they moved. Big cases were always coming their way, so they decided to get an office in the middle of the city.

Jason began to read the article out loud. "A talented young detective, Jason Streak has yet again solved an almost impossible case. With the help of his partner, he was able to solve the case. What seemed to be an unsolved murder, turned out to be nothing more than a cakewalk for these talented young detectives. This case required more than brainpower, Jason pursued the accused Kevin Brown across town. During the chase Jason had to jump through a glass pane, just to stop the perpetrator," Jason slammed the paper down on the table, "it was two, two glass panes. Can't these people get anything right," Jason stammered in disbelief.

"The media likes to twist things around," Ryan said while gazing out the window.

Jason picked up the paper and continued reading the article out loud, "This isn't the first case that the NYPD deemed unsolvable that the young detectives managed to crack. When asked, Commissioner Pavel Anosov had this to say 'It's great to see that there are young people willing to take action in keeping our city safe. I feel that their influence will be beneficial for the police department," Jason stopped reading and looked up from the newspaper.

Suddenly the sound of nails on a chalkboard filled the room as the door to the office opened. A beautiful young woman wearing an oversized red hat looked in.

"Excuse me, where can I find Jason Streak?"

Jason stood up, cleared his throat and started walking towards her, "I'm Jason Streak," he said while extending his arm.

"Oh," her face looked perplexed as she shook Jason's hand.

"Is something wrong? I mean of course something is wrong, why else would you come to a detective agency. It's just that your expression shows some concern."

"I guess what I've been reading about you is true. Truly, you are a master detective," she said with a smile "I just didn't expect you to be this tall."

"In my case, the camera sheds a few inches. Have a seat so that we can chat," He points to the chair, and led her to it.

She sat down, putting her purse on the desk. She also noticed that Jason was reading the paper, "Checking your horoscopes, detective?"

"It says that I will meet a beautiful young woman today."

"Hopefully my horoscope is as good as yours detective," she said as she shot Jason a smile.

"I'm actually just reading about a recent case that we solved. People love reading this kind of junk. Write anything down and someone is bound to believe it."

"Are you saying that I shouldn't trust the media's opinion of you?"

"That depends. What does the media say about me?"

"Well let's see, master detective, a genius, no unsolved cases, always happy to lend a hand and a master detective"

"You said master detective twice."

"From what I hear you are very good at what you do. So Jason, tell me, is the media right about you?"

"Even though they sometimes get certain details incorrect, they seem to paint a decent picture of me."

Ryan sat down on the couch, "You mean details of you and your little Hollywood chase," he commented while scrolling through his notebook, trying to find a blank page.

Jason looked at him with a smile. "That's my partner, Ryan. For some reason, he is also my best friend."

"That's me alright," Ryan said without lifting his head from his notebook.

"The news did mention that you had a partner. I'm guessing that's you, Ryan."

"Did they say anything good about me," Ryan asked as he looked up from his notebook.

She took a moment to remember, "Not really, they just mentioned that Jason had a partner. They failed to mention your name."

Ryan laughed, "Don't worry, that's the life of a sidekick."

Jason interrupted their little chat, "Public perceptions aside, I still don't know your name."

"Jessica. Jessica Holmes."

"Nice to meet you, Jessica," Jason said, "So are you a well-known figure yourself?"

"No, I'm just a regular girl, in need of some help."

"Well, you came to the right place."

"Good to know," she smiled.

"Jessica, so what brings you in today? What sort of problem are you having?"

"Nothing really, it's…. This might sound a bit stupid, but I don't feel safe."

"That doesn't sound stupid to me. Why don't you feel safe," asked Jason, who was now sitting at the edge of his seat.

"There's this guy that's been following me. I think he might be a stalker."

"Well I can see why he would take an interest in you," Jason blurted out without thinking, "I'm sorry if I made you uncomfortable with that comment. I didn't mean it like that. We just happen to get these types of cases a lot."

Jessica couldn't help but laugh at his comment. She was aware of the fact that she was a beautiful woman, "So should I go on?"

"Of course, share any information that you think might be of use."

"Whenever I go to the mall to get coffee, I see him. I don't know how long he's been doing this, but I noticed him about two weeks ago."

"Are you writing this down Ryan," Jason asked him.

"No, I'm just drawing cartoons. Of course, I'm writing this down," Ryan answered sarcastically.

"Sorry, do go on," Jason said.

She nodded, feeling somewhat uncomfortable. Talking about the matter brought many unpleasant ideas to her head. What if this person planned to kidnap her, or they wanted to rape her? She hated thinking about it, but she knew that if she hired Jason, he would definitely help her.

"About two weeks ago, I began to notice a hooded figure with a camera. At first, I thought little of it, but recently wherever I go in the mall he is there. I tried asking the security officers at the mall for help. They just laughed at me and told me to settle my domestic problems like an adult," Jessica began to sob a bit, "I don't know what to do anymore."

Jason wanted to press on for more information but decided against it.

"Don't worry I fully understand your situation. I would also be terrified if I was in your shoes," With those few words the client calmed down a bit and reached for a tissue, "To get a better grasp of the situation, I need a little bit more information, such as a description of the person."

"I never got a good look at his face. But, what I do know is that he always wears a hooded sweater. Whenever I see him he's is always wearing dark colors."

"That really narrows down our list of subjects," Ryan snickered.

"Do you have any idea who this person might be," Jason said as he gave Ryan a dirty look, "Is there someone that would want to harm you, like an ex-lover?"

"None that I can think of," she said reluctantly.

"Look, Jessica, when we started out these

cases were a dime a dozen. In almost every case the clients tell us the truth. They all just happen to leave out a couple of key details. So Jessica is there anything that you are forgetting?"

"Well, there was one thing. A couple of days ago I found a couple of pictures in my mailbox," she said while looking at her feet.

"What kind of photos were they? You did mention that the person had a camera," Jason asked as he stood up.

"They were candid photos of me. Some of the photos were taken at the mall, but some," she paused, her eyes began to water, "some of them were taken of me at home."

"So we are dealing with a stalker. Jessica, can you leave me your phone number and address?"

"My address and my phone number is that all? What will you do now?"

"I'm going to formulate a plan of action. Actually, I have a meeting that I must get to. But this case is my top priority that I can assure you."

"Oh okay, so when should I expect to hear from you?"

"Very soon, don't you worry about anything Jessica, these kinds of things happen every day. My partner and I, always exceed our client's expectations. That's what we do."

"I do hope that you exceed my expectations," she said as she picked up her bag and stood up, "212-233-5727 is my number. I live on 1727 Cardinal Avenue. I'll be expecting your call Mr. Streak," She shot Jason a warm smile as she walked towards the door. The detectives couldn't resist checking her out as she walked out the office. Her tight red dress, that matched her gigantic hat, highlighted her figure perfectly.

"You got her number written down Ryan?"

"Yup, I have her digits written down right here," Ryan said as he pointed at his notebook.

"She said Cardinal Avenue right?"

"Yeah, she said Cardinal Avenue why?"

"Ryan it seems that we have another important case to solve."

Ryan looked at him confused, "Did you just say that we have a case? Don't tell me you are actually going to take this case."

"Why wouldn't we take this case," Jason said while taking Ryan's notebook from his hands. He quickly flipped to the page with Jessica's information. He made sure that he added her to the contact list on his phone.

"Jason, we deal with actual crimes now. Since when did we start taking these types of cases again?"

"Ryan, we started taking these types of cases when we signed up to be detectives. Are you honestly telling me that you felt nothing from her story," Jason asked as he tossed the notebook back at Ryan.

"Jason, we both know that what you felt had nothing to do with the case. You just want a reason to spend time with her."

"True, but it is a simple stalker case. You know that this case will be a walk in the park. Can you really blame a guy for wanting to spend time with that?"

"Jason she is smoking hot but don't let that cloud your judgment. This case sounds easy, but I'm sick of these kinds of cases. I want us to put real criminals away. She should just call her father, brother or boyfriend to solve this giant mystery."

"Who said you'll be wasting any of your precious time on this case? This case is being worked on by yours truly. She did come in looking for me you know."

"Sure, whatever, have fun on your little romantic case, but be quick. Who knows when a real case might show up?"

"Don't you worry Ryan, this case will be done in a jiffy," Jason opened his desk drawer and grabbed his wallet, "I'm heading out for a bit, make sure to let the painters in when they show up."

"Going on a date already," Ryan snickered

"Let's not get ahead of ourselves; I'm just meeting with an old friend."

CHAPTER 2

Jason had to take about three different trains to get to his meeting. The meeting place was a bar in Brooklyn that could pass as a condemned building. It wasn't the first time that Jason had entered this establishment, but he wished it was his last. The bar somehow managed to look worse than the new office did. Saying that it was rundown would be a compliment. You could tell that the owner did not care about attracting new customers. Jason's friend loved this specific bar, but Jason loathed the place. Other than the regular drunks, the place was always empty.

"Like always, you're late," said a voice from the bar.

"I'm so sorry Commissioner Pavel, please don't arrest me," Jason sarcastically responded as he took a seat next to the commissioner," Barkeep I will have the same thing he's drinking."

"How come whenever you say commissioner it loses all its flair," The bartender placed Jason's drink in front of him, "I'll be taking that," Pavel said as he grabbed Jason's drink. Before Jason could react the commissioner had downed it.

"Can I get a double of your best single malt scotch neat," out of the corner of his eye he could see the commissioner ordering himself another drink, "Don't forget that all my drinks go on his tab."

This time Jason was actually able to receive his drink. Unlike Pavel he wanted to enjoy his drink so he sipped at it, "So what are you drinking Pavel?"

"Vodka, I grew up drinking it and god knows

I will die drinking it," Pavel laughed as he said his joke.

"Why, is it because you're Russian?"

"Of course"

"So what made you want to see me?"

"Can't I spend time with my favorite detective? Also nice work on the homicide case, I'm proud of you and Ryan."

"At least we were able to save that girl," he said taking another sip.

The commissioner remained quiet.

"She did make it, didn't she?"

The commissioner took a drink and shook his head.

"Dammit! What more can I do," Jason slammed his fist down on the bar, spilling some of his whiskey.

"Don't beat yourself up over it son. You did your part. You caught him."

"It just gets me that throughout the whole chase, he pleaded he was innocent. But look at what that monster did. Just look at all the bodies he piled up."

"We don't know what goes through criminal minds. Sometimes they will say anything to seem innocent."

"You would know. How long have you been doing this, fifty years?"

"Only thirty years! I can still teach you a thing or two," Pavel commented as he ordered another round of drinks.

Jason looked up at the ceiling. He couldn't get Jessica out of his head. He felt that there was a connection between them.

"How was it, back in Russia," he asked Pavel, trying to get his mind off Jessica

"Russia was a war torn nation. Sometimes when I close my eyes I can still see it, houses on fire, the sounds of women and children screaming. My best friend died in my arms, had to use him as cover. A bullet split his head in two and the blood splashed onto my face," he shuddered as he retold the story. His hands shook as he went to grab his drink. They calmed down after he had ingested the alcohol, "you are lucky Jason. Your father did the right thing, moving to the States before the war reached your city."

"I don't know if that was the right decision. When I hear these stories, I think that it would have been better to fight for our country. He just ran away like a coward. Who knows what the outcome could have been if we stayed?"

"The war was horrible. I would not wish my experiences upon anyone. Your father's number one priority was his family. He knew that staying meant almost certain death."

Jason took out his wallet, "This round is on me. Two more drinks."

"Leaving already? The party just started, I didn't even tell you my kidney stone story."

"I actually have a new case," the bartender brought them their drinks.

"Work, you still haven't recovered from the last case," Pavel said while grabbing his drink.

"Just a bit of pro bono," Jason said as he threw his drink back.

"I didn't know you were the generous type. I should get you to do some pro bono work for the city."

"I think you've had enough to drink."

"We put another criminal behind bars, we should celebrate," Pavel said as he raised his glass, signaling the bartender to bring another round.

"No. I'm at my limit, plus I'm working a case right now. I can't show up at the client's house stumbling, now can I?"

"I understand. Next time bring Ryan down here, I've always wanted to see him drunk."

"I'll ask him to come next time," Jason stood up and gave Pavel a friendly hug before heading out.

Once outside, Jason began admiring the neighborhood. It wasn't the cleanest neighborhood, but the buildings were beautiful. Brownstones as far as the eye could see, each standing the test of time. As Jason walked through the streets of Brooklyn, he passed abandoned factories. Half a century ago this neighborhood was the place to be, now not so much. There was one factory that made Jason stop in his tracks, the old McGregor Factory.

The closed down factory was Jason and Ryan's first "big" case. The case also brought the detectives in contact with Pavel who was a police captain at the time. Four years ago, the factory was used by a serial killer to stash the bodies of his victims. The killer targeted middle-aged women. He had his way with them and then disposed of the bodies in the factory. Jason and Ryan were hired to find a missing mother; they found her dead inside of the factory. After contacting the police of their findings, Jason and Ryan were hired as consultants on the case. The serial killer which had run rampant for half a year was brought down by Ryan and him in a week.

Jason started walking again. Halfway down the next block, he grabbed his phone from his pocket. He was tempted to call Jessica, but he was nervous. Jason began to imagine how the media would tell his story. NYC's best detective scared to talk to the opposite sex read more about it on page three. Jason laughed at the thought. Everyone believes that detectives have their pick when it came to the opposite sex. The clients are usually dealing with the loss of a loved one or a cheating spouse. Jason and Ryan were constantly working cases, so his social life was nonexistent. For some reason Jason felt, he had a connection with Jessica. He has spoken to hundreds of clients on the phone, but he has never been this nervous before. This call wasn't so much about the case but rather personal.

The case wasn't only about catching the stalker, but also seeing if there is a connection between him and her. "I have delivered heartbreaking news to clients, this call is nothing compared to that," Jason said to himself in his mind. After his little affirmation, he scrolled through his contact list and tapped on Jessica's number. He immediately regretted his decision, after three rings he ended the call.

As he was about to put the phone back in his pocket, it started ringing. The number that was calling was none other than Jessica.

"This is Jason," he answered the phone

"Oh. Hi Jason this is Jessica, I just missed your call and decided to call back."

"I was actually calling to set up another meeting. Do you have time to meet up now?"

Jason took out his keys and started twirling

them. He often did this when he became nervous.

"I actually wanted to go the mall to pick up a couple of things."

"That actually works, I'll see you soon," Jason hung up his phone and began walking to the nearest corner. Luckily when he arrived at the street corner, a yellow cab pulled up to the curb. As soon as the passenger got out, Jason jumped in.

"Where to sir," the cab driver asked as he began to drive

"1727 Cardinal Avenue, Dean."

"Have we met before? You do look familiar."

"No, I simply read your name off of your medallion. My job requires me to be a very observant person."

"What do you do for a living?"

"I'm just a simple private investigator."

"I knew it, but I can't believe it. You are Jason Streak!!!"

"Guilty as charged," he said while he handed Dean one of his cards.

"This is the first time that an actual celebrity has been in my cab. Do you need me to turn on the air conditioning because you seem to be sweating quite a bit?"

Jason took out his phone and looked at his reflection, "Can you turn it on, if you don't mind. I must be sweating from some whiskey I had earlier."

Dean set the air conditioner on max, "So are you working another big case? Am I actually driving you to a crime scene?"

"No nothing like that. It's a smaller case, yet I feel a bit nervous."

"A master detective such as you is getting

nervous? Do you want to talk about it? I've been told that I'm a good listener."

"The client, she's a... It's hard to explain but it should be a simple case."

"Just a simple case of the butterflies," Dean started laughing hysterically.

"Don't quit your day job, Mr. Comedian. I'm just a bit out of practice."

"Just go with the flow. Don't over think it, have no set agenda. Whatever happens, happens don't set any expectations."

"I'll be sure to try it out," Jason said as the cab arrived at Jessica's house.

The house was located on the corner of the block. It was an old brownstone, that was built back in the twenties. Like all other houses in the city, it was attached to the adjacent building. The door had no doorbell, just a brass knocker.

Jason decided to call her, "Hey Jessica, I'm downstairs"

"I'll be right down."

Jason's palms began to sweat. To help calm himself, he took out his keys and twirled them. While twirling his keys, he decided to check his emails.

"I don't think that your keys work here."

Jason turned his head to see Jessica smiling in the doorway. She was now wearing a blouse and a pair of blue jeans. He quickly put his keys and phone back into his pockets, "I wasn't trying to open your door or anything like that"

"It's just a joke. So are you ready to go?"

"Do you mind, if I use your bathroom"

"Sure no problem third door on the right."

Jason ran inside the house. The last thing he

wanted was for him to need the bathroom in the middle of the investigation. While on his way to the bathroom, Jason began to notice the little things around the house. A picture of a blue dress caught his eye. Once he opened the bathroom door, the smell of lavender filled his nostrils.

The whole ordeal took only a few minutes, "Thanks for letting me use your bathroom."

"No problem, so do you want to drive to the mall or walk there? I'm parked a couple of blocks over."

"I think we should walk there, it will give us time to talk," Jason walked down the stairs onto the sidewalk, "So, what's your favorite store in the mall?"

"That's your first question? I thought you would ask me what I did for a living, or how could someone like me afford a brownstone in Manhattan? You are a weird one Mr. Streak," she said, as she joined him on the sidewalk.

"I often find, that when you ask a question that someone is not expecting, they will usually answer a question that wasn't asked. If you want to tell me about yourself, then feel free. But before you do, please stop with the Mr. Streak. You are making me feel like an old man."

"I design women's dresses for a living and my favorite store in the mall is Lisa's Boutique on the third floor. Whenever I go to the boutique, I get to see the joy in a person's eye as they try on my creations. Might sound a bit girly, but their joy brings me joy."

"So, was that red dress this morning designed by you?"

"No, I never wear anything that I design, it

would make me feel weird."

"Other than visiting Lisa's Boutique, what else do you do in the mall?"

"I usually just go to the Coffee Hut in the food court; I can spend an entire day there."

"I take it that they offer free Wi-Fi."

"They do, but it's not the only reason I can spend an entire day there. I get to see what people are wearing, gives me inspiration. So Jason, what is your plan?"

"I don't really have a plan per say. Each case is different so there is no set plan of action."

"Do you think that you will be able to help me? We never spoke about payment for the case."

"Don't worry; I will be able to take care of this. Once this case is done, just write me a check for whatever you feel is fair. I haven't taken a stalker case in over a year, so I actually don't know how much to charge."

"If you haven't taken one of these cases for so long, then why did you happen to take my case?"

"I saw a person in need of help. I don't want to see your life get ruined by something so trivial. I just need you to trust me, just go along with whatever I say. Jessica, are you able to do this?"

"Jason, I do trust you."

"Okay because the stalker might be watching us at this very moment. Don't turn around, if he's here then let him be. What I need you to do is, to pretend to be my girlfriend."

"Wait why do I have to pretend to be your girlfriend?"

"A lot of stalkers think that they have a chance with their prey. By pretending to be your boyfriend, the stalker should give up on you."

"What if he doesn't stop, what would we do then?"

"If this doesn't work, then we would go with plan b. Don't worry, I will handle this for you. You have my word."

After hearing Jason's statement, Jessica stopped and turned to face him. She wrapped her arms around his neck and gave him a kiss. Once their lips were no longer locked, she started to walk again.

Jason was dumbfounded; it took him about twenty seconds to recollect himself. He went into a little jog to catch up to her, "What was that for?"

"Just felt like showing my thanks to my boyfriend, is there anything wrong with that?"

"No, there's nothing wrong with that," took him a second but Jason finally understood why Jessica kissed him. Jason had done this fake boyfriend plan many times before, but this is the first time that he was kissed out of nowhere.

Jessica could see that Jason was still a bit flustered, "Let's go grab a coffee."

"Are we here already," Jason turned his head towards her. Right in front of him was the mall, "Sure let's grab a cup of coffee."

"I didn't know my little kiss would affect you this much. The great Jason Streak brought to his knees by a kiss."

"Sure laugh, I was just lost in thought," he said as he held the door open for her. "Lead the way."

"Sure," she said while trying to grab his hand, Jason quickly pulled his hand away "Remember we are a couple. So we have to act like one."

Jason grabbed her hand and walked through

the front door. As Jason walked throughout the mall, he felt as if his neck was burning from all the dirty looks he was getting. Once they reached the escalator, Jessica turned around to face him.

"How are you holding up?"

"I'm fine, why wouldn't I be?"

"You just seem a bit nervous, that's all," She said as she walked off the escalator.

"Sorry about the sweaty palms. I had a couple of drinks before meeting up with you. My body is just sweating the alcohol out. Do you think the great Jason Streak gets nervous?"

"I'm a bit nervous, is there anything wrong with that?"

"No, there's nothing wrong, with being nervous. I was just trying to say, uh," Jason was at a loss for words.

Jessica wrapped herself around Jason's arm, "It's so fun to mess around with you. I wonder if your girlfriend has as much fun doing this, as I am," she whispered in his ear.

"Not tied down at the moment. I wonder what your boyfriend would say if he knew you were here with me."

"You just want to know if I'm single don't you," she said as she ran her finger through his hair, "Let's go order our coffee, how do you like yours?"

"I take my coffee black without sugar, why?"

"Go find a seat, I'll get the drinks. Don't worry I won't be long."

Jason could not help but admire Jessica as she walked away. He decided to message Ryan. His text was simple and to the point, it read "How did the day go," Jason was about to put his phone away when a call from Jessica came in.

"Just got the drinks, did you find a place to sit?"

"I'm right in front of the fountain."

Once Jessica arrived at the table, Jason got up and pulled her seat out for her. At the same time, he was surveying the area for the stalker. One person, in particular, caught his eye. He was sitting alone with a satchel on top of the table. To watch the person, he positioned his chair perfectly across from him.

"Sitting a bit close are we, not that I mind"

"Just want an optimal view of the area," Jason said as he took a sip from his coffee, "By the way what did you get."

"A Frappuccino, and don't try to change the subject. I saw the way you looked at me in your office."

"With my eyes," Jason jokingly asked.

"You think I didn't notice. Why else would the best detective in New York take my case?"

"I would love to answer your question, but I will be right back," Jason said as he stood up. He took one last sip of coffee before going into a full sprint towards the suspect. Jason had watched the suspect take photos of him and Jessica.

As soon as the suspect saw Jason start running, he turned tail and headed towards the escalator. He ran up, throwing people out of his way. Jason decided to chase by running up the down escalator. Luckily the suspect was out of shape so he easily caught up to him.

"Stop following my girlfriend, or else," Jason shouted right as he got within five feet of the suspect.

"I'm sorry; I didn't know she was taken.

Please just let me be, I promise that this will never happen again," the suspect responded in a trembling tone.

"Yeah right, why should I believe you?"

"I promise," the suspect cried out as he ran towards the entrance of the mall.

Before Jason could respond or catch up to him, a mobile cart appeared out of nowhere. He couldn't avoid crashing into it, so he just put his arms up to shield his face. A loud crash sound filled the entire mall. After landing on the ground, Jason felt a sharp pain on his right side. To his dismay, he was unable to get up without assistance.

"Jason honey, are you alright," Jessica shouted as she ran to him,

"Did anyone happen to get the license plate of that car? It came out of nowhere," he said sarcastically as Jessica helped him up.

"Sir my cart is ruined! What is going to become of this," The cart owner asked while throwing his arms up in the air.

"Send a bill to my office," Jason said as he handed the cart owner his card. He looked at his right side and saw blood coming through his shirt, "Jessica let's go home,"

"Yes, let's go home."

Jason tried to walk on his own but began to stumble, "Jessica, can I borrow your shoulder."

"We need to get you to a hospital. You might have a concussion."

"I'm alright; remember you said that you would trust me. Let's just take a taxi back to your place. I just need to take a little breather."

Jessica's face showed concern, "Okay let's

go," she put his arm around her and helped him to the door. As soon as she was outside of the mall she saw a cab pull up. Right, when she was about to enter the cab, a man in a suit tried to take the cab for himself.

"Excuse me, I was getting in."

"Listen here missy, I am a busy man and need this cab. You and your drunken boyfriend can wait for another one."

"Prosecutor Pallone, you sure think highly of yourself. What makes you think that I am drunk?"

"Mr. Streak I didn't know that was you. Let me help you into your cab. Also, your girlfriend looks very lovely."

"Thanks but no thanks," Jason waived the prosecutor away. He was able to sit down in the back seat on his own.

"1727 Cardinal Avenue," Jessica told the cab driver as she got in, "Jason, what were you thinking? What if he had a weapon?"

"I'm sorry; I didn't fully think things through. On a side note, I don't think you have to worry about him anymore. I think that little chase did the trick."

Jessica sat there quietly. She then crossed her arms and turned to face the car window.

In less than ten minutes they were in front of Jessica's house. Jason swiped his card and walked out the cab. Jessica was standing in front of the door.

"Would it be too much to ask to come inside for a bit?"

"I don't know it's getting kind of late. I have to get up early in the morning."

"I fully understand, I just thought that you could patch me up," he said as he lifted his hand from his side. Jason had bled so much that, blood was dripping from his shirt."

"Oh, my god, Jason come inside quickly. Did he hurt you? Are you bleeding anywhere else? Why didn't you tell me earlier?"

"No, he didn't hurt me. This is a wound from when I jumped through the glass panes. I didn't want to worry you about something so trivial."

"Why would you offer to help me when you are clearly in no condition to work? Let's go inside," She led him inside, "Sit down and I'll come back in a second."

"Sure, by chance do you have any whiskey?"

There was no answer from her. Jason dug his phone from his pocket and saw that the screen was cracked. It seemed like nothing was going his way today. He failed to apprehend the stalker, opened up his stitches and Jessica hated him.

To Jason's surprise, Jessica came down with a bottle of scotch and a sewing kit. She handed Jason the bottle of scotch, "For you and your wound. Take off your shirt; I need to see how bad it is."

As soon as he took off his shirt, the sewing kit hit the floor. Jessica's face looked as if she had seen a ghost.

"It's not as bad as it looks, just opened up a couple of stitches. Why don't we do this in the kitchen? This way I don't get blood on your furniture and we can sterilize the needle."

She just nodded and led him to the kitchen. She also handed him a wet paper towel, so that he could clean around the wound. Right before she was about to sew in the first stitch, Jason flinched.

"I'm sorry that I jumped. I just have a thing about needles," He said as he took a sip of scotch from the bottle.

"How can you be afraid of needles? You are New York's most fearless detective. I bet you that you wouldn't even feel the prick of the needle."

"I've seen hundreds of needles, they are evil. Also who wouldn't feel the prick of a needle; it hurts worse than a paper cut."

"Apparently you aren't able to feel it. I'm already on the third stitch."

Jason looked down and saw the needle and thread sticking out from his skin. Just the sight of the needle sent shivers through his body, "Just let me know when you're done," he said while taking another sip from the bottle.

After half an hour and half a bottle of scotch, Jason wound was fully sewn shut. Jessica was now dabbing the area around the wound, to remove any remaining blood. When she began cleaning the wound, Jason let out a small grunt.

"Are you alright?"

"I'm fine; I just have a few bruised ribs."

"Is it from when you collided with the cart," Jessica asked as she grabbed the bottle of scotch from him. She took a drink from the bottle, "Now that you are stitched up, you shouldn't move around as much. We wouldn't want the stitches to open up again."

"I bruised my ribs working another case last week. Crashing into the cart just made them hurt a bit. It's getting kind of late, I should head home."

"Since you never finished your coffee, I was going to make a pot. If you have to go, then I understand."

"I can never turn down a cup of coffee. Do you remember how I take my coffee?"

"You take your coffee, straight out of the pot into the cup. Go have a seat in the living room; I'll bring it out to you when it's done."

Jason walked back into the living room and sat down. He wanted to put his shirt back on, but it was stained with blood and a bit torn. He decided it was best to leave the shirt off. He pulled out his phone to see if Ryan had responded to his message, "That's weird."

"What's weird," Jessica asked as she walked in with two coffee mugs. She handed Jason his coffee and sat down next to him.

"It's weird that I haven't heard back from Ryan yet. I wanted to see if the workers finished fixing up the office. If it still smells like paint, then I'm not going in tomorrow. This is why I didn't want to move our office."

"So why did you move your office into the city? Where was it before?"

Jason took a sip from his coffee, "Our old office was in the middle of nowhere, Staten Island. Moving to Manhattan was Ryan's idea; I would rather have just stayed there or moved to Brooklyn."

"Staten Island, your old office was there. I'm surprised you had any clients, to begin with."

"That was also Ryan's idea. I wanted to have the office in Brooklyn, but he wanted to pay close to nothing for rent, so we ended up there. Thinking of that ugly office makes me want to finish that bottle of scotch. Let's change topics, why live in a brownstone?"

"I inherited it from my parents," she took a long drink from her coffee, "They passed away in a car accident, five years ago. Their entire estate was left to me, so I decided to stay in this old house. Call me sentimental, but I think they would have wanted me to live here rather than selling it."

Jason heard a crackling in her voice and saw tears forming in her eyes, "I think they would have wanted you to live here too. I lost both my parents also, my mother passed away when I was little and my father passed when I was seventeen. Ryan's family took me in, treated me like I was their own son," This time there was tears coming out of his eyes. He quickly grabbed his blood stained shirt and used it to wipe his face.

"I'm sorry, for your loss."

"Hey, it's all in the past. We can't change our past, so we just have to learn to live with it. Jessica you have my condolences. Thanks for the coffee but I should really get going," he finished the rest of his coffee in one sip.

"Do you live in Manhattan?"

"Nope, I'm a Brooklyn boy. I live in Brighton Beach."

"Why don't I just give you a ride home? It's only twenty minutes away."

"I don't want to impose. You stitched me up, gave me whiskey and made me the best coffee I have ever had. I'll just take a cab."

"Taking a cab with that bloody shirt, I'm no detective but that sounds like a bad idea. Let me just change my blouse and then we'll head out"

"Jessica, if you're insisting then sure."

Jessica grabbed both coffee mugs and walked to the kitchen. After dropping the mugs in the sink, she walked back to the living room. She grabbed her purse and headed towards the stairs. While walking up the stairs she stopped halfway, "I think that we might be banned from the mall. So you have to help find me a new place to get coffee."

"Sure, just let me know when you want to go looking for one."

She just smiled, Jason smiled back at her. She continued walking up the stairs in silence. Once she was out of sight, Jason decided to take a shot from the bottle of scotch. After taking the shot, he decided to rest his eyes. He knew that it would take her some time to change outfits. In no time, Jason was sound asleep.

"What time is it," Jason said out loud as he was woken up by the vibration of his cell phone. He grabbed his phone and saw that it was nearly eleven pm. "Hey, Jessica are you alright? It's been over a half an hour. I can just take a cab."

There was no answer. Jason thought that she might have decided to take a nap like he did. Jason decided to go upstairs and check on her; while walking up the stairs his phone began vibrating again. He tried answering it but the broken screen wouldn't allow him to do so. Once he reached the top of the staircase, he felt a breeze. Other than the breeze there was a door that was cracked open with some light shining through. As he walked towards the door he noticed that the hatch to the roof was open. Instead of walking to the door he went to inspect the ladder that lead to the roof, there were fresh blood droplets on it.

He quickly took out his phone and unlocked it with his fingerprint. "Call Pavel," he said to the voice control on his phone.

"Jason where are you? I have been trying to get in contact with you for a while now," Pavel shouted.

"Whoa calm down a bit and listen. I need you to send a squad car to 1727 Cardinal Avenue, I think…"

Before he could finish, Pavel cut him off, "Jason there are some squad cars on their way already. We received an anonymous tip, that a young girl had been attacked in her house. The description of the culprit matches you perfectly. What is going on?"

After listening to Pavel, Jason ran to the room with the slightly open door. He swung open the door and almost fell back in horror. Jessica was lying in the middle of the master bathroom in a pool of her own blood.

"JASON! Are you there!? Don't tell me this phone dropped the call!"

"I'm still here. Send an ambulance, Jessica has been stabbed. I think she might be dead. I'm going to check for a pulse now."

"Do not touch that body! Get out of there now the police are on their way. Find a way out. Someone is trying to set you up; we can fix this as long as you are not behind bars."

"I'll contact you when I can. For now sit tight, try not to lose your job commissioner," Jason hung up the phone and knelt down next to Jessica's body.

"Jason is that you," Jessica asked in a faint voice.

The sounds of police sirens filled the air, "Yes Jessica it's me, Jason. I'm going to find whoever did this and make them pay. I need you to stay with me okay. Remember we need to find you a new coffee shop. I'm going to go get help; can you do me a favor and promise me that you will wait for me or the police?"

She moved her head up and down slightly in acknowledgment. Jason gave her a kiss on the forehead and walked out the room. He ran down the corridor to the ladder. As soon as he took his first step on the ladder the police started speaking on a megaphone.

"Come out with your hands up!"

"Jessica, I'll be back for you. I promise," he shouted. Jason ran up the ladder. Lucky for him all the houses were connected, so he was able to run across them. Once he reached the roof of the furthest building, he used the voice controls to call 911.

"911, what's the emergency?"

"A man in bloody clothing came up to me and said that she's alive. He looked like that detective that's always in the news. After telling me this he ran into the subway. It looked like he came from the direction of Cardinal Avenue," Jason hung up the phone and threw it as far as he could.

He looked over the roof to see if there was any safe place to jump on. There was nothing but pavement and parked cars. Jason without hesitation jumped off the roof.

CHAPTER 3

Jason landed on the ground with a loud thump. Right, when he took his first step, pain shot through his body. The impact of the fall was a too much for his body to handle in its condition. Jason knew that he had to get out the area no matter what. Without hesitation Jason began sprinting, he had no set destination. The pain was excruciating, but it was nothing compared to jail time.

Jason ran for about ten minutes before the pain became unbearable. In those ten minutes, Jason had traveled about a mile and a half from the crime scene. He needed to get out of the city fast before anyone called in an anonymous tip. Being a famous detective was actually working against him. He decided to sit down on the curb so that he could come up with a plan.

Jason had a couple places that he could hide out at; the only problem was reaching them. He was a wanted man: almost everyone in the NYPD was after him. Since it was so late at night, he had no way of getting a disguise. No phone and no means of transportation made him a fish out of water.

As Jason got up to begin his journey a cab pulled up across the street. Jason thanked the heavens; it looked like his luck was changing for the better. He hobbled across the street. He opened the back door of the cab and got in.

"So did you get over your butterflies, sir?"

"Holy crap, Dean is that you."

"Yes. I usually do a twelve-hour shift on Fridays. I heard on the radio, that the police are looking for you. They are actually offering a reward for information about your whereabouts," the sound of the doors locking filled the cab.

"Listen, Dean whatever you are hearing on the radio is untrue. What they are saying I did is a lie. I would never hurt her; someone is trying to frame me. If I am taken in for questioning, I can guarantee that whoever attacked her will walk. I need to solve this case, no matter what. Neither you nor the NYPD will stop me, you understand."

Dean could sense that his passenger was ready to overpower him at any moment, "Mr. Streak, it was all in good fun. I am a good judge of character. I can sense that you did not commit any crime. So where would you like me to take you?"

"Can I really trust that you will not give up my location?"

Dean turned off the cab's meter, "You can fully trust me, so where to?"

"I need some cash, so can we stop by a bank. Just park a block away from the bank, wouldn't want them catching your plate number."

"What bank do you use," Dean asked as he started driving

"I use Chase Bank, of course."

The rest of the ride went by in complete silence. Jason was busy trying to come up with a plan. He and Ryan had an outdoor storage unit in Brooklyn, that was registered under Jason's old pet's name. They set up the storage unit after they started taking on dangerous cases. Ryan made Jason promise that he would only use the unit when they needed to hit the mattresses. Ryan loved to use phrases from The Godfather.

Dean stopped after making a left onto a one-way street, "The bank is two blocks down. I can wait here for you or I can leave, it's up to you."

"I'll be back trust me. I can't get to where I'm going by foot."

Jason was lucky that it was so late at night. No one was walking the streets, so he didn't have to worry about getting identified. He speed walked to the bank. He quickly slid his card into the door slot and opened the door. The max he could take out from the ATM was a thousand dollars. Hopefully, that was all he needed, because it was only a matter of time before his account was frozen.

Within five minutes, Jason was back in the car. Dean turned to the shirtless detective, "Where to?"

"Can you take me to Paul's storage on the corner of Bedford Avenue?"

"Why, a storage facility"

"It's a safe house of sorts. Both my partner and I have a change of clothing, a couple of burner phones, some canned foods, and some pocket money."

"Wow, sounds like something out of old crime movie. I didn't think that detectives had safe houses."

"Working high profile cases brings us lots of negative attention. We get anything from death threats to actual attempts at our lives. This safe house has saved our skins multiple times. I just can't believe that I have to use it for a simple stalker case. I mean this job was supposed to be quick and easy."

"Sometimes in life, the easy road turns out to be the hard road."

"Look at you, you're both a philosopher and a

comedian," Jason jokingly said, as he tried to lighten the mood.

"I do have my masters in psychology."

"Wait. Do you really have a masters in psychology?"

"You have to learn not to judge a book by its cover. Just because I drive a cab, doesn't mean that I'm not educated."

"So what made you want to drive a cab?"

"It's a long story, probably longer than your story about tonight. Also, I don't think your safe house is as safe as you think," Dean said as he stopped for a red light.

"What makes you say that?"

"The three police cars on this block, not to mention the two undercover police standing on the corner."

Jason began to look at his surroundings. Dean was right; there were at least eight officers in the area. He was sure that no one knew about the storage unit other than Ryan and himself, "Keep driving, I have somewhere else that no one knows about. One of the storage workers must have seen me use it in the past and reported it to the police."

"What makes you think that this other place will be safe?"

"Not even my partner knows about this place. If the police somehow manage to find me there, then God must truly have something against me."

"So, where are we off to now?"

"Staten Island, if you want I can put the address in your phone's GPS."

Dean handed his phone to Jason. A few moments later Jason handed it back to him along with two hundred dollars.

"What's this for," Dean asked while counting the money.

"It's a little something to show my gratitude. Not many people would have helped me in my current situation, but you did Dean. You, my friend, are one of the few people that I can rely on in my time of need."

"My gut tells me that you didn't do it and my gut is almost never wrong."

"Why do you say almost never wrong?"

"It sometimes tells me to have Taco Bell and that never ends well."

The two shared a quick laugh. When they reached the Verrazano Bridge, Jason had to pretend to be asleep in the back seat. He did not want to attract any attention from the police at the toll booths.

"So aren't you going to ask," Jason asked Dean.

"Ask what, about the situation with the police?"

"No, I was expecting you to ask how the 'date' went."

"If the entire police force is chasing after you, then I can assume that it didn't go that well."

"Wasn't it the great philosopher Dean of the yellow cab, who said, don't judge a book by its cover. Other than Jessica getting stabbed, the NYPD manhunt for me and me destroying a mall cart; the 'date' went surprisingly well," Jason said as he let off a nervous laugh.

"So my advice did help out with your butterflies. That's good to hear. Is this the place?"

"Yup, this is it. See not a single police car in

sight."

"I do not doubt that there isn't a single police car in sight because this is an orphanage. Your secret safe house is an orphanage."

"It was either this or a graveyard. The graveyard wouldn't be a good idea on Halloween, so I chose this. No, but seriously, I know the priest that runs this orphanage, he was my father's friend. I need you to ring the doorbell and ask for Father Montgomery."

"Wait, why?"

"I don't know who is going to answer the door. I don't want some random nun or worker calling the police. If they say to come back in the morning, tell them that it's a matter of life and death that you speak to him. I'll be behind a tree listening in."

Dean walked up to the front door of the orphanage and rang the bell. Jason was right around the corner, hiding behind a tree. It took a couple of minutes before someone answered the door.

"Sorry, for waking you up so late at night. But I must speak with Father Montgomery, it's a matter of life and death," Jason heard Dean say.

"I am Father Montgomery, what can I assist you with?"

"I need to stay here for a while," Jason said as he emerged from the shadows.

"Jason is that you? I've been hearing terrible things on the news all evening about you. I haven't been able to sleep because of it."

"Don't worry father, none of it is true"

"If any of the things they said were true, then your father would be rolling around in his grave.

Jason's friend would you like to come on in for a cup of coffee?"

"I think I should be going, I have a busy day tomorrow. Jason, take this it has my number," Dean said as he handed Jason a card. After that, Dean drove away into the darkness.

"Jason come in before anyone sees you out here."

Jason followed the father inside the old building. Jason was surprised at how little had changed at the orphanage, since his last visit. The paintings on the wall to the plastic covered couches appeared untouched. Even the wax fruits seemed to have the same layer of dust on them.

"I take it that you want to go straight to bed," Father Montgomery said as he walked up the staircase at the end of the hallway.

"It's been a long day. Don't worry we can have a nice long chat about it in the morning. By chance is my suitcase still in the room."

"The room has not been touched by anyone other than me since your last visit."

"Thank you. If possible wake me up around nine am and when you do bring lots of painkillers. I'm going to need them."

As soon as they reached a door at the end of the hallway, the father handed Jason a key. Right after Jason grabbed the key, the father walked back towards the way they came. Jason put the key inside the keyhole and unlocked the door to room seventeen.

The room was rather empty; there was only a bed and a nightstand with a lamp. On top of the bed was a medium sized suitcase. Jason walked to the nightstand and began emptying the contents of his pocket on top of the nightstand. He decided to turn on the lamp and closed the door locking it behind him. The suitcase could wait so he placed it on the floor. He lay on the bed with no pillow or blankets. He decided to take a look at the card that Dean had given him. He looked at the card and laughed.

It was his own card, with Dean's number scribbled on it. Jason couldn't believe that in less than twenty-four hours his value had dropped so much. One minute he was a celebrity the next he's America's most wanted. There was nothing more that he could accomplish tonight so he decided to turn in. After turning off the lamp he closed his eyes and passed out.

CHAPTER 4

After a short night of sleep, Jason was awakened by pain coursing through his body. He staggered to sit up, his ribs were killing him. He did not feel the pain last night because of an adrenaline rush. Jason grabbed the suitcase and opened it up. Inside the suitcase was a change of clothes, a cell phone, and a wallet. Jason counted the money in the wallet; there was seven hundred dollars in the wallet. He then plugged the cell phone into the wall to give it some juice. In less than a minute he had the phone up and running. Jason dialed number 2 from the speed dial.

"Voyeurs Corp," answered a voice.

"Stiggy, is that you?"

"Who is this?"

"I can't say my name over the phone. The Runaway Russian or whatever the news is calling me. Stiggy, I have a job for you."

"What do you need?"

"The mall by Cardinal Avenue in Manhattan, I need you to pull the surveillance footage. I was in there towards the end of the day. I ended up chasing a guy from the food court to the escalators and crashed into one of those carts. I need to know everything about the guy I was chasing."

"So name, address, and background the usual?"

"Yes, but I need it soon, very soon."

"Why don't you have your friend the commissioner do this for you?"

"I can't get him involved at this point in time.

So how much for this, remember I can't access my accounts."

"How much are you able to pay."

"I can pay you five hundred now and the rest after we take care of everything."

"Once I get the information I will call Ryan to set up the meeting."

"No, I'll text you this number, just call me back here. I don't know if anyone is screening his calls, so try to keep this between us."

"Full secrecy, I understand."

As soon as Jason was done with the call, he heard a knock at the door.

"Come in, I'm decent"

The door opened and to Jason's surprise, a nun walked in. He was expecting Father Montgomery, not a nun that he had never met. Hopefully, the father did not spill the beans.

"Sorry for the intrusion, I was told that we had a guest staying with us. So I just wanted to introduce myself and see if you needed anything from us. Also, I brought a bottle of water in case you were thirsty."

"Thanks. I'm Jason," he said as he stood up and walked towards the sister with his arm extended out.

"It's a pleasure to meet you, Jason, I'm Sister Christine. If there is anything else you need feel free to ask," she said while shaking Jason's hand. She then handed him the water bottle.

"Do you by chance have any pain killers?"

"Oh my, I forgot them downstairs. I will go and get them, just give me a couple of minutes."

"Take your time; I'm going to go take a shower. So you can just leave them on the nightstand."

"Do you need me to show you where the shower room is?"

"No, you don't have to. I know my way around the orphanage. By the way, where is the father?"

"He is currently conducting the morning sermon. You are free to join us if you want. That is after you finish showering."

"I might do just that."

Sister Christine left the room and Jason walked back to the bed. He grabbed a change of clothes from the suitcase and headed out of the room. He walked down the hallway and towards the bathroom. Every step he took made him hate walking, because it felt like he was constantly getting punched in the side. Right before the bathroom was a little closet filled with towels and washcloths. He grabbed one each and proceeded to enter the bathroom.

It took only ten minutes for Jason to be done with his shower. When he returned to his room, he noticed a container of pain relievers on top of the nightstand. He quickly opened it and took out three pills. Jason swallowed the pills without water; he hated taking them with water. Jason grabbed the cellphone and decided to attend the morning sermon.

The chapel was attached to the orphanage and could fit around a hundred people. Even though the orphanage was a bit rough on the eyes, the church was properly maintained. The first two rows of seats were filled with children ranging from the ages of three all the way to late teens. Jason counted about fourteen children in total. Since the sermon was already underway, Jason decided to sit in the back.

"Do unto others as you would have them do unto you," Father Montgomery's voice resonated throughout the chapel, "This is how we all must live our lives. We must treat our neighbors with the utmost respect."

As Jason sat there listening to the sermon, his pocket started to vibrate. He grabbed the phone from his pocket and saw Stiggy's name show up on the caller ID. Jason immediately got up from his seat and walked out the chapel.

"That was fast. What did you find out Stiggy?"

"I have the stuff, but why get paid peanuts when I have the golden goose. The police are paying three times what you are. All I have to do is provide them information on your whereabouts, so I need you to make this worth my while."

"Stiggy, are you kidding me? You know the situation I'm in. Are you really going to try and shake me down? If you try and take me down, you will also be taking yourself down. Some of the stuff that was swept under the carpet might appear."

"It was just a test, to see how serious you are about this. I can bring you the stuff on one condition."

"Stiggy, what's the condition. My back is to the wall."

"I want Ryan to come to the meeting with the rest of the payment. Your situation is a bit rocky. I just have to worry about myself and my employees."

"Like I said before, I don't know if they are bugging the phones. I have no way of getting in contact with him."

"Don't worry I will take care of getting him there. Just meet me under the bridge, Jersey side of course. In two hours."

"Make sure he isn't tailed."

"Just be there," with that the call was over. Jason dug his free hand into his pocket and pulled out the card that had Dean's number. He dialed the number and to his surprise, it went straight to voicemail.

"Hey Dean, this is Jason. Sorry to bother you so soon. I kind of need another favor; I need to get to New Jersey. I need to get there in two hours if you cannot do it, I understand. Call me back on this number if you can."

After leaving the voicemail, Jason decided to listen into the remainder for the sermon. He took his seat in the back of the chapel, the sermon only lasted a couple of minutes but it was refreshing. The few minutes of the sermon that Jason heard was enough to make him forget about his problems. Father Montgomery's words had a tendency to speak to a person's soul.

"Do you want something to eat? Before we talk that is."

Jason was so lost in his thoughts that he failed to notice that Father Montgomery had taken a seat next to him.

"You know you shouldn't sneak up on a wanted criminal."

"You are just like your father. No matter how bleak the situation, you both keep your sense of humor through it. If you're not hungry we can head straight to my office."

"I am restricted on time. I need to be in New Jersey in a little under two hours. So I have to figure out if Dean is able to bring me there. So I think we should just talk in the kitchen."

"I can always drive you," Father Montgomery said sincerely, as he stood up from his seat. The two of them walked out the chapel.

"I know you can drive me. I don't want to inconvenience you or any of the nuns here."

"Jason, I promised your father that I would always be there for you. You know that I am on your side, please trust me."

"My situation is bad, father its real bad. This meeting could be a trap, for the first time in my life I'm scared. I always have a plan, but for this I can't formulate one. There are too many variables and time is of the essence. If I take too much time the killer will have more time to get away and the chances of the police finding me will increase."

"Why go to this meeting, especially if it could be a trap? Aren't you in good relations with the commissioner," he asked as he opened up the door to the kitchen.

"The person who is framing me might have a few officers on the payroll. You know how corruptible New York's finest can be," Jason grabbed a bagel from the bread box, "the purpose of the meeting is for me to pick up some information."

"Is the information worth the chance of you getting caught?"

Jason took a bite of his bagel before speaking, "the information could help me solve this case. The person getting the information is somewhat reliable. The only problem is I don't know if Ryan can lose his tail."

"What do you mean his tail?"

"The police are watching the office, so if

Ryan leaves they will surely have a squad car or two tailing him. This is exactly why I didn't want to get Ryan involved in the meeting."

"I understand. So tell me, what actually happened yesterday."

Jason grabbed a bottle of water from the fridge and sat down on a stool. He then proceeded to tell Father Montgomery of the events from the prior day. Jason did his best to not leave out any details.

"So do you have feelings for her, or are you afraid of losing another victim."

"It's a mixture of both," Jason as he finished his bagel.

"If she does not pull through you cannot blame yourself. Whoever did this to her would have hurt anyone as long as they knew that they could frame you for it. You help protect God's children from harm and you do that well. All we can do is leave her in God's hands. If she is meant to live she will it's all based on his will."

"That's easier said than done. When I saw her lying in a pool of her own blood, I …" Jason was cut off by the phone in his pocket ringing.

"Go ahead and answer it. I will be right back," Father Montgomery said as he walked out the kitchen

"Hello," Jason answered the call.

"This is Dean; I just got your message."

"Sorry for taking advantage of your kindness, but are you able to drive me around today?"

"No problem I can drive you around to wherever you need. I won't be able to get to you for about an hour."

"Crap, no problem. Are you able to meet me in New Jersey? Also how much to be my chauffeur for the day?"

"No cost, I'm not doing this for the money. After this mystery is solved, I will have the peace of mind knowing that I made a difference in the world. Where do you want me to meet you in New Jersey?"

"I will text you the address of a park. I will meet you there. I won't be there right away; I will be picking up some information from someone in the area. I don't know if police will be there so just have your phone ready because I will call you when I'm headed to you. Thanks again, Dean."

"No problem, I will be waiting for your text and call."

Once the call was over, Jason paced back and forth in the kitchen. He had a means of transportation for after the meeting the question was how he was going to get to the meeting. After pacing for all that time, the pain in his side began hurting and Jason was forced to hunch over the counter in agony.

"Good you're still here. Were you able to get a ride to the meeting?"

"Nope and to make matters worse the painkillers are losing their potency."

"Don't worry, you still have plan b."

"What's plan b, I didn't even know we had a plan a."

"Sister Christine will drive you to the meeting. I already informed her that she might have to drive to New Jersey. Don't worry I told her you were a pastor returning from a mission. I told her that she just has to drop you off at a church that's a three-minute walk from the meeting place. Also, put these on, we can't have you dressed like a civilian," Father Montgomery said as he handed Jason a pastor's robe, a clergy collar and a pair of sunglasses.

"I'll go change right now; you really came through for me."

"You can only get so far by relying on yourself. Even when times are rough I will always be here to lend a helping hand. Now go on hurry up, the clock is ticking."

Jason limped his way to his room. Before changing into the outfit he popped a couple of pills. Changing into the outfit was difficult because of the pain but the pills kicked in before he was done. After he was done changing he put on the sunglasses and put the bottle of painkillers in his pocket. He walked down the stairs and out the front door. He was greeted by Sister Christine standing in front of a Toyota Camry.

"Are you ready to go, Father Jason?"

"Yes, I am, Sister Christine," Jason knew that he would probably go to hell for impersonating a priest. But it shouldn't be that big of a sin because it was asked of him by a priest. Jason thought to himself as he entered the car. He laughed at the idea. If he failed to solve this case, he will go on a real mission. The only problem it wouldn't be a mission in a developing country. It would be a mission to Rikers Island.

CHAPTER 5

Sister Christine barely spoke as she drove Jason to New Jersey. Jason had a hunch as to why she was silent. He needed to keep as many people on his side as possible. If his hunch was correct then he had to fix the situation before things went south.

"Sister, I take it by your silence that you know who I am."

"You are Father Jason," the Sister said as she kept her eyes on the road. She had not made eye contact with him the whole car ride.

"I'm talking about who I really am."

"Of course I know who you are. All the nuns at the orphanage know who you are. Father Montgomery has clippings all around his office. You are Jason Streak, the wanted super sleuth."

"Father Montgomery told you that I was a priest to protect you. He doesn't want to get you involved. I know that I am a burden to everyone in the orphanage, do you think I wanted this. Father Montgomery could get charged for harboring a fugitive."

"It is not my place to judge. I can only complete the task which I was assigned. If possible I would like to end this conversation. I do not wish to further incriminate myself."

"I'm going to end the conversation but let me just say this. Let him who is without sin cast the first stone. The sister that I met this morning lived her life by that proverb."

Jason wasn't expecting an answer from the sister; he just wanted to make her reflect on her actions. Good thing that they were only blocks away from the church. If she took his words to heart, then she would see that Father Montgomery had her best interest at heart.

The car pulled up in front of a run-down church in Elizabeth New Jersey. Jason got out and walked towards the church. He made sure that he didn't make eye contact with Sister Christine. He walked to the church and leaned on the gate; he grabbed his phone and dialed Stiggy. There was no answer, this made Jason worry. There was still no indication if he was walking into a trap or a normal meeting.

As Jason walked through the streets of New Jersey, he tried his best to stay alert. He made sure to walk slowly and scan the area for any person that seemed out of place. With every block Jason walked, the more he felt that he was acting a bit paranoid. After walking around five minutes, Jason decided to try Stiggy again, but there was still no answer. Jason knew that if he called Ryan he would get an answer but then he could no longer use the phone. Was this meeting worth throwing away his only means of communication? Being overcome by stress Jason took a seat at the curb and took out his keys. As he twirled his keys, Jason decided to take out the phone and call Ryan.

The universe had other plans for Jason, as soon as he started dialing Ryan, a call from Stiggy came in. He immediately picked up the call.

"Stiggy, I was wondering when you were going to call me."

"Seems you are back to your cocky self, is that why you aren't here yet?"

"Don't worry I'm in the area, I was just waiting for you to arrive. You took the tunnel here; the bridge would have been faster. The question is where Ryan is," Jason asked as he stood up and began walking again.

"So you're keeping tabs on me."

"Stop looking around to find me and answer my question. You told me that this meeting was not going to happen unless he was present. I'm just following your rules," With this statement, Jason was able to put the ball in his court. He used his inference skills to gain knowledge of the situation. Since multiple calls to Stiggy's phone went straight to voicemail, it meant that he took the tunnel to New Jersey. By Stiggy refusing to answer Jason's question about Ryan meant that Stiggy was alone. Because Stiggy dealt with information gathering he was a bit timid. So Jason was able to give off the illusion that he was there watching him.

"He's on his way, no need to get defensive."

"It's my life on the line, not yours. I will see you when he arrives," with that Jason hung up the call. It was moments like this that Jason wished he had a flip phone. Just so he could flip the phone closed to make ending of the call more dramatic.

Within twelve minutes, Jason was at the meeting place. He made sure to stay out of sight so he was hiding behind a dumpster. The dumpster smelled so bad that it almost made him puke, but it was the only hiding place that served as a good vantage point. The meeting place was a parking lot behind a rundown industrial office building.

Stiggy had used the parking lot many times to meet up with the duo. Jason had observed Stiggy's behavior in each of their many meetings that he picked up on a couple of his habits. Stiggy parked in two different places depending on the situation. If he had one of his employees observing or listening in from far away he parked by a light pole. If he had no one listening in or watching him he would park close to the water. For this meeting, Stiggy had parked near the water, so that meant this meeting would be between the three of them.

Twenty minutes had passed and still no sign of Ryan, so Jason decided to call Dean. After two rings Dean picked up the call.

"Hello, Mr. Streak."

"Hey Dean, I'm just calling to see how far you are from the meeting place."

"I am getting on the bridge now as we speak, sir"

"Dean you have to drop the sir and Mr. Streak. You're making me feel old."

"Sorry about that, sir."

"We will work on that later. I will call you once I start heading towards you," Jason hung up the call and peaked out from behind the dumpster. Stiggy was still the only one in the parking lot. To kill his boredom, Jason decided to take a peek inside the dumpster. As he lifted the cover slightly, the stench hit him straight in the face. The smell actually made Jason throw up a little in his mouth. As Jason was trying to send the vomit back down his throat he heard a car horn.

A car had just pulled into the parking lot. It was a blue Honda and it parked a couple of spaces away from Stiggy. Ryan emerged from the car and he immediately looked around the area. Jason quickly layed down on the floor; he knew that Ryan was an observant person. To Jason's dismay, a person that he had never seen before also emerged from the car. He quickly pulled out his phone and called Stiggy.

"Look who's calling, it's Big Brother."

"I don't like being Big Brother but you're leaving me no choice. This was supposed to be a meeting between the three of us. I didn't check off plus one on my invitation, you are the one that needs to get paid, not me. So either you get rid of him or I walk."

"I'll get rid of him."

"I'll see you after I'm sure that no one else is around," Jason once again hung up abruptly. After hanging up, Jason decided to walk around the building so that he could approach the parking lot from the side of the water. Through speed walking, the entire trip only took a couple of minutes.

"Hey Ryan, did you miss me," Jason asked as he stepped into the parking lot.

"Jason, did you just come from the water and what's with that getup," Ryan asked while looking Jason up and down.

"Just got finished baptizing someone in the harbor," Jason jokingly said as he approached Ryan and Stiggy.

"Enough with the small talk, let's get down to business," Stiggy chimed in. "It's pretty windy out there, let's talk inside my car."

"That's a good idea, I call shotgun then," Ryan said.

"Nope, there's no need for us to talk. I just need the information," Jason said without moving.

"Jason, why are you acting so cold towards us,

we just want to help you," Ryan said as he took a couple of steps towards Jason.

Jason took a step back, "Ryan, just look at my situation I don't know who I can trust. Heck, I don't even know if the police are listening in. If I get in that car there's a chance that the child safety locks are set to on. It doesn't matter how low the probability is, I have to stay on my toes."

"We are just going around in circles. Let me get the stuff it's in the car," Stiggy walked to the trunk of the car. Within thirty seconds Jason had a manila envelope full of papers in his hands.

Jason quickly looked the papers over and it looked like everything was there. Jason dug into his pocket and pulled out a small wad of cash and handed it to Stiggy.

"Ryan, pay him the rest, I have to start working on this," Jason said as he lifted up the envelope.

"Wait, Jason are you working this case on your own? Do you know what kind of position you have put me in? I was down at the precinct for an hour this morning getting interrogated about you. Let me help you fix this, stop treating me like a sidekick."

"Position that I put you in? Are you kidding me Ryan, you were interrogated for an hour? You got to leave after that and last night you were able to sleep in your bed in your apartment. I'm looking out for you Ryan, if someone is coming after me, then they could be coming after you. When I feel the time is right then I will fill you in," Jason turned his back to his partner and began walking away.

"Jason! Jason, come back we need to talk," Ryan screamed across the parking lot.

Jason's decision hurt him more than it hurt Ryan. Jason knew the fewer people involved the better. Even though the decision was the right one, it still made Jason feel like crap. He had to turn off his personal feelings because he had a case to solve and little time to do it in.

In no time, Jason had reached the park where Dean was parked. Jason looked around the park and did not see any yellow cabs. Jason dug his phone out of his pocket and immediately dialed Dean.

"Hello, sir. I see that you have arrived."

"Just got here, Dean where are you parked, I don't see the cab?"

"I'm parked right at the corner. I'm in the Ford Taurus."

"Ford Taurus, Dean are you sure that you're not a cop."

"I can assure you that I am not one of New York's finest. Plus I look bad in blue."

"See you in a couple of minutes," Jason hung up and walked to the direction of Dean's car. Once at the car, he opened the passenger side door. Jason took his seat and turned to Dean. Jason was silent, but his face showed off how impressed he was with the car.

"Don't tell me that you thought I only drove a cab. So where are we off to sir?"

"We are off to meet the man who holds my future in his hands. He might be the key to solving this crime or he might be the mastermind behind it all."

"Okay… but where?"

"We are going to 170 Broadway in Manhattan and if you can, step on it."

CHAPTER 6

Jason reached for the car radio and changed the station to 106.7. Dean shot him a look, but Jason ignored the look and raised the volume. Jason loved to listen to music while working on a case, it helped him concentrate. This current case was no exception.

"106.7 lite FM, I would not have pegged you as one of their listeners?"

"I love slower music. I would have chosen cd 101.9, but they took that off the air years ago," Jason said as he flipped a sheet of paper from the envelope.

"You keep looking over those papers. Are they clues or something," Dean asked.

"These papers might lead us to a clue relating to the perpetrator or to our prime suspect."

"Well, are you going to share with the class or not?"

"This right here is a background check for a Mr. Jose Rogers."

"Am I supposed to know who that is? I'm new to this detective stuff can you give me a better hint," Dean asked as he lowered the volume of the radio.

"Mr. Rogers was the reason why Jessica hired me. He's a man who became infatuated with Jessica, for good reason I assure you. He has been stalking her for quite some time."

"I understand why he might be the prime suspect but how can he lead us to the perpetrator?"

"Well when I chased him through the mall, he promised to stop stalking Jessica. He might be skeptical of my relationship with Jessica. The reason for this is because he was stalking her for a couple of weeks and this is the first time he has seen me with her. In which case, he might have been watching her house or had a hidden camera capturing photos."

"Hidden camera? What makes you think that he has a hidden camera?"

"Jessica mentioned that she found candid shots of her at her home. From the angle of the photos, it is safe to assume that Mr. Rogers was not standing outside of her house snapping the photos."

"But sir, what if he did stay true to his word? Wouldn't that mean he was not present at the time of the attack?"

"That would be the case if he didn't have a hidden way of taking photos of her. So if my little scare tactic set him on the right path, then he might have come back for the camera. If I'm lucky his camera might have caught the real criminal on it. On a side note, just Jason will suffice."

As the car drove along in silence Jason began to think. There were a few different ways that his face to face with Jose could go. Jason had a tendency to cover all the possible outcomes of any given scenario. By doing this he ensured that he would never get taken by surprise on a case. Last night was, of course, the exception.

"Dean, I'm going to need you to drop me off a block away from the address. In the meantime can you find parking and text me the location?"

"Don't you need me to go in and back you up? You know, just in case he tries to get physical with you."

"From my previous interaction with him, it would seem that I can handle him alone."

Dean dropped Jason off a block away from the

address. Before letting Jason out, he shot him a look of concern. Jason would love to let Dean come in and help but he couldn't. His methods of interrogation might be a bit too intense for the cab driver. In only a few scenarios would Dean's presence be beneficial. As Jason walked up to the building he couldn't help but notice that the door was locked and there was an intercom system in place. Luckily for Jason as he approached the door someone was walking out of the building. He quickly made his way into the apartment complex and walked his way to the stairwell. Jason wanted to be on as little surveillance as possible.

Jason opened his envelope and let out a sigh. Mr. Rogers lived in apartment sixteen B which meant Jason would have to walk up sixteen flights of stairs to reach the apartment. A quarter of the way up he had to pop a couple more pain killers. The walk up the stairs wasn't the hard part, doing it with bruised ribs and a wound was. By the time Jason reached the sixteenth floor he was no longer holding his side. The painkillers worked but it seemed that they worked less and less as time went on.

Jason knocked on the door of apartment sixteen B, but there was no answer. He knocked again and still no answer. Jason surveyed the area making sure no one was around after he was sure he was alone he pulled out his wallet and got on one knee. From his wallet he took out a small lock picking set and went to work on the door's lock. Jason always kept a lock picking set in his wallet for such an occasion. In less than a minute, Jason had the apartment door unlocked. He quickly rushed into the apartment and closed the door behind him.

The apartment was dark, all the lights were

off. Jason found the nearest light switch and flipped it on. He then walked around the apartment trying to understand the way the mind of Mr. Rogers worked. He looked around but the place was spotless, there wasn't even a stack of mail on the table. This could mean only two things either Mr. Rogers was a neat freak or that the killer had gotten to him first. Jason was hoping that it wasn't the second one; in the meantime, he grabbed his phone and saw the text from Dean. Jason turned off the lights and sat down to wait and see if Mr. Rogers would return to his apartment.

Time flew as Jason sat in the dark, when he grabbed his phone to check the time; he saw nearly three hours had passed. Since that much time has passed he decided to use the bathroom. Because he walked through the apartment earlier he was able to navigate to the bathroom with minimal lighting. Jason made sure to throw some water on his face, to help wake him up. As he was about to walk out the bathroom, Jason heard the locks on the door unlock. Before Jason could get back to his seat the door swung open.

Jason waited for the door to close and the lights to come on before leaping from the bathroom. He quickly rushed to the person who entered the apartment and covered their mouth so that they wouldn't scream. He looked at the face of the person; it was the stalker Jose Rogers.

"Listen, Jose, I'm going to remove my hand from your mouth. I need you to promise me that you won't scream. I just want to ask you a couple of questions. Can you do that?"

Jose nodded his head up and down. Jason

released him and pointed to the nearest chair. Jose was silent as he walked to the chair.

"Who are you, Mr. Priest? Take anything you want please don't hurt me," Jose squealed in terror.

"Don't you recognize me, wow this disguise is pretty good," Jason commented as he removed his sunglasses. "We had such a good jog yesterday, remember?"

"It's you, Jessica's boyfriend. I swear that I don't know anything about what happened last night. I stopped stalking her just like I promised."

"Calm down a bit okay, but when did I ask about last night. I know you were there last night, tell me what you saw. Jessica's life is on the line, I need any information that you have."

"Sorry, but I didn't see anything."

"Jose, do you realize what's at stake here? The attacker might come after you next. Look at how easy it was for me to find you, the person behind this is a monster. They are trying to frame me for murder, who knows what they might do to a witness. The decision is yours to make, just think it through."

Jose sat in the chair quietly; he looked down at his hands. Jason walked towards the door. He looked over his shoulder, but Jose was still silent. Right, when he opened the door he heard a faint "wait". Jason closed the door and turned around to see Jose standing up.

"Sit down, I'll tell you everything," Jose said as he sat back down, "I was there last night, but only to remove my equipment. When I got there, I saw her stitching you up and decided to take some photos. The lighting and composition was perfect. Before I knew it time had flown by, you were already sleeping on the couch. I was about to put away my camera when I noticed a person on the roof. I took some photos of the person, I have the pictures right there in my camera," he said as he pointed to a bag on the floor.

Jason stood up and walked to the book bag; he picked the bag up and handed it to Jose. Jose pulled out a digital camera from inside the bag. The camera was a big DSLR with a long white lens and a flash attached.

"Did you have the camera setup just like that?"

"I don't understand."

"Jose was the L lens and flash attached to the camera when you took those photos last night?"

"It was dark; I needed them so that I could take the photos. For a camera to be able to take photos at night, having a fast lens and a flash help out a lot," Jose said as he turned the camera on.

"I know how cameras work; I am a private investigator after all. Where did you shoot your photos from?

"I took the photos from the roof across the street why? I don't see why that matters."

Jason stood back up and grabbed the camera from out of Jose's hands. Jason quickly flipped through the recent photos and suddenly stopped. He looked up slowly from the camera. He then handed the camera back to Jose, "Get some clothes and pack your camera gear. We need to get out of here now!"

Jose took a look at the photo that made Jason antsy, it was a photo of the culprit looking and pointing in his direction. He almost dropped the camera, his hands were shaking.

"Jose, I know you're scared right now, but I'm going to make sure no harm comes to you. So trust me and just follow my instructions. Grab your camera gear, some clothing, any cash lying around and that is all. Leave your cell phone and any other electronics here. Do you have these photos saved on any computer or anywhere else?"

"No, I haven't moved them onto my computer yet. To gather my things is going to take me at least twenty minutes."

"Well you have less than five minutes," Jason pulled out his phone and called Dean, "Dean, we need to get out of here quick. I'll be down in about seven minutes."

"I'll be there sir don't you worry. See you then."

"Just so you know, I will be bringing someone along for the ride," Jason hung up the phone and walked towards the front door. Jason took his keys out and started to twirl them. It was a good thing that he went over all the possible scenarios in his head, because he was prepared. It wasn't the best scenario, but it was still manageable. Jason had a photo of the suspect and an eye witness. He was used to working cases with barely any clues, so this was a major break through, "I'm leaving now, if you don't come with me then I wish you luck," Jason yelled out loud as he opened the door and closed it as if he had walked out.

Immediately Jose ran out from his room. He was holding a duffel bag with clothes sticking out, "Why would you do that, I'm almost ready. Just give me a couple of more minutes."

"We need to leave now, or else we lose our window of opportunity to avoid this person. They might be on their way here; it's too early for me to meet them."

Jason reopened the door and walked out. He was already behind schedule and couldn't afford to spend any more time in the apartment. He put his keys back in his pocket and pressed the button for the elevator. Shortly after pressing the button, Jose stumbled out of his apartment.

"Were you really going to leave me in....." Jason had to cover Jose's mouth.

"Keep your voice down. We don't want to cause a scene, be as quiet as possible. Just follow me and try not to bring attention to us," Jason said as he removed his hand from Jose's mouth.

"You know you can just put your finger on your lips, rather than covering my mouth," Jose said as the pair walked onto the elevator.

Jason did not reply to Jose, he remained quiet throughout the elevator ride. As soon as the elevator reached the lobby he rushed out. In less than a minute he was outside the building looking for Dean's car. The sound of a car horn pointed him in the right direction.

"Where to sir," Dean asked as Jason and Jose entered the car.

"We are going back to where we first met."

"The mall," Jose asked from the backseat.

"I wasn't talking about where I met you, Jose. I'm talking about where Dean and I first met. Brooklyn…"

CHAPTER 7

"So what's in Brooklyn," Jose asked from the back of the car.

"A friend, that might be able to help me identify the culprit. Are you able to transfer the pictures from your camera to a smart phone using WIFI?"

"Of course it can, why? You made me leave my cellphone at my apartment."

"Dean, is it alright if I save a couple of photos onto your phone? I want to have a copy, because we will be handing the memory card over to my friend."

"Sure, here's my phone sir," Dean said as he pulled his phone from his pocket.

"Wait why are we handing my memory card to your friend," Jose butted in.

"Didn't I ask you to trust me? My friend is more than likely the only person who can help us identify the culprit from a photo. He can also cross reference the photo with everyone in the NYPD database. It might not look like it but Jason Streak always gets his man."

"NYPD database is your friend going to hack into the police database. You might be a wanted criminal, but I still have a future. I can go back to school and get my degree or even start a YouTube channel. But I cannot go to federal prison," Jose said as he transferred the photos onto Dean's phone.

"Are we really meeting with a hacker, sir?"

"No, we are not meeting with a hacker. I already met with one this morning. That's how I got your information Jose. We are going to meet with a good friend of mine that happens to work for the NYPD. The plan is nearly perfect, we hand him the memory card and wait for him to give us a lead," Jason said as he raised the volume of the radio.

Jose leaned over the center console and lowered the volume on the radio, "What do you mean the plan is nearly perfect? Also by helping you out wouldn't this friend put their job on the line? It seems to me that you are hiding some information from us. All three of us are in the same boat, this affects all of us."

"All of us are in the same boat, not at all. Jose, you just have to lay low for a couple of weeks and then your life would go back to normal. Dean can easily go back to his normal life. If I don't solve this case, then my goose is cooked. A guilty criminal would escape and I would get sent to jail. Since I put away many criminals, I could easily lose my life in jail. The friend that I want to drop the memory card to is the Commissioner of the NYPD. Getting in contact with him will be hard part. Since we are close, he might have internal affairs watching him. His calls are definitely being screened."

"If he is under surveillance how are you going to hand him the memory card," Jose asked as he handed Jason back the cell phone.

"The commissioner loves the sauce. After his wife passed away he has been going to the same bar every night. Drowns his pain away with work and alcohol it's a sad sight; however it makes our job a whole lot easier."

"That sounds easy enough, but how will you know if he is being watched in the bar?"

"Jose, do I really have to break the whole plan down for you? You're going to go in first to sniff out any cops. If the place is clean, then you will let me know and I will come in."

"Why can't Dean go in? I don't know how to spot an officer. If I make a mistake you could go to jail. I'm not feeling well all of a sudden," Jose began to hyperventilate.

"Jose calm down, you're hyperventilating. Dean's job is to drive around the area and make sure that it is safe. He is also our driver, so he has to stay with the car. Your job is real simple; you just walk in and see if anyone is sticks out. The bar isn't classy and an officer should be easy to point out. Basically anyone in a button up or polo would stick out in there."

"So you want me to walk in, and then walk right out? Won't that make me suspicious?"

"Not exactly, I'll explain it to you while we walk to the bar. Right now I just want to rest until we get there," Jason said as he ingested some painkillers.

"Walk! We are in a car right now why do we have to walk there. What if the attacker is in the neighborhood and sees us?"

Instead of responding, Jason reclined his chair and got comfy. He closed his eyes and took a quick power nap.

In no time Jason felt a nudge. He opened his eyes to see the old McGregor Factory to his right. The clock on the radio read six pm.

"Sir, while you were asleep I explained to Mr. Rogers the reason behind walking to the location. I will survey the area and call you to tell you my findings.

"Thank you, Dean. Jose can you pass me the memory card," Jason asked as he unbuckled his seatbelt. He turned to the back seat and grabbed the memory card from Jose.

Within minutes, both Jason and Jose were outside the old factory. The weather was cool with a soothing breeze. It was the perfect weather for a walk. Because of all his injuries, Jason was walking rather slowly. The painkillers helped somewhat but each step that he took was met with a small jolt of pain.

"You know I'm truly sorry about what happened. I can't believe there are people out there, who would do such horrible things," Jose said as they reached the corner.

"This factory was used by a serial killer to dump the bodies of his victims. What I learned in this line of work is that you can never underestimate a person. I've seen some pretty dark things, but this is the first time that it has affected someone close to me. If she doesn't pull through, the image of her limp body on the bloody bathroom floor will haunt my dreams," Jason said as he caught up with Jose.

"Don't worry she will pull through and we will catch the person behind it."

"Thanks, I needed that. So was this the first time you stalked someone?"

"I know that's how it looks, but trust me it isn't what it seems. I am a freelance photographer and I've been trying to build a portfolio. It's hard to explain but when I saw Jessica, I knew she was the perfect model. I would have asked her to be a model but look at her, then look at me. Someone like that is out of my league, you're living proof. Best detective in the city, how can an average Joe compete with you?"

"I'm also an average Joe just like you. I'm not a celebrity or a hero; I'm just a regular person who thinks out of the box. You just need confidence; I'm in the same boat as you."

"Same boat, you are going out with Jessica. You have a career that you are proud of. I am a struggling artist trying to make it in the big city."

"My detective agency didn't become number one overnight it takes time. No one saw Ryan and I when we only ate ramen for over half a year so that we could pay our bills. Do you know what this fame has done to me? It has made me a wanted man and has hurt an innocent woman. I know that the work I do brings justice to the world but at what cost?"

Jose stopped walking and turned to face Jason. His jaw was wide open; he couldn't believe what he was hearing. In front of him was a man who many saw as a hero, bearing his soul.

"Let's keep walking we're almost there," Jason said as he caught up to Jose. The two continued to walk in complete silence. Jason stopped a block away from the bar, "Jose, this is how you will signal me letting me know if it's safe for me to come in," he said as he pointed to a pay phone.

"Is that a pay phone? How do we know that it works," Jose asked as he walked towards the pay phone.

"Like this," right then the pay phone started ringing.

"How did you do that?"

"This pay phone can receive phone calls. Once you survey the area, call this payphone to let me know if it's safe for me to come or not. Since I just called the payphone, the number is saved in the call history," Jason said as he handed the phone to Jose.

Jose grabbed the phone and placed it in his pocket. He walked down the block alone to the bar. Within minutes he was entering the bar.

Jason stood right next to the pay phone, waiting for the call. He stood there for a couple of minutes, before he started pacing back and forth. As he paced he dug his hand into his pocket and brought out the pain killers. Jason tried to take three pills out but only two came out. He looked inside the bottle and saw that is was empty.

"How am I out of these already? I need to buy some that actually work," as Jason said this to himself the pay phone rang. He picked up the receiver, "Hello," he said. Jason listened to Jose talk on the phone, "I'll be right in," he said and immediately hung up the phone. Jason placed the empty bottle on top of the pay phone and walked in the direction of the bar.

Jason walked into the dimly lit bar and spotted Jose sitting at the bar, just a seat away from the commissioner. Jason sat down in the empty seat between the two. The bartender saw that Jason had sat down at the bar and walked towards him.

"What can I get you father? Wine?"

"I really shouldn't be drinking because I'm on medication but screw it. Can I get a double of your best single malt scotch neat?"

Commissioner Pavel turned around in his seat, "It can't be, Jason is that you?"

"It took you long enough, commissioner. So how's work?"

"Don't ask me how work is. Didn't I ask you to lay low; you don't even know if I am being watched. This is not the time to play hero, let the police handle your case," Pavel said as he took a sip from his drink.

Jason grabbed his drink from the bartender, "No offense commissioner, but I can't leave the case to the police. If I did leave it to the NYPD then I wouldn't have a picture of the culprit right here in my possession."

"Jason, do you really have a photo of the culprit," Pavel shouted as he jumped off the bar stool.

Jason just sat there, drinking his whiskey. He did not even turn to face the commissioner. Jason took out the memory card and placed it on the table.

Pavel grabbed the memory card from the table and put it in his pocket, "How do I know that this is actually a photo of the culprit?"

"It might not be the cleanest photo but you should be able to find some new suspects from it. I'll call you tomorrow to follow up with you," Jason finished his drink, left a twenty dollar bill on the table and started to walk out of the bar.

Pavel followed him out the bar, "Jason, just so you know, she's out of critical condition. Don't try and visit her, she is being guarded. Just please listen to this old man's request, just this once."

"Commissioner, don't worry I will only do what's right. Do I look like someone who will disobey an order?"

"That's what I'm afraid of," commissioner Pavel as he walked back into the bar.

CHAPTER 8

Jason waited for Jose at the payphone. Within a matter of minutes, Jose's silhouette could be seen walking in Jason's direction. Before Jose even reached Jason, his voice echoed through the empty streets of Brooklyn.

"Why didn't you tell me that you were instructed not to work on this case? Right now other than being the prime suspect you are making the entire police force your enemy," by the time Jose was done talking, he was standing in front of Jason.

"Jose, don't tell me that you actually agree with the commissioner? If I left this case up to the NYPD, then I would be the one behind bars. I was able to find clues about the real attacker. The evidence that I found is photographic evidence, which will clear me from being a suspect. By meddling in this case, I am doing more with my limited resources than the NYPD with all of their manpower. Hand me the phone, so that I can call Dean."

Jose handed him the phone, "I'm sorry if what I said offended you in any way. The media paints this picture of the police being the ultimate crime solving machine. This is the first time I get to look at what really happens behind the scenes of solving a crime."

Jason texted Dean their location and sat down on the curb, "Jose, I'm sorry that I snapped at you like that. The commissioner wanted me to get out of Jessica's house as soon as possible. I decided to check on Jessica to see if she was still alive and she was. By him telling me that she is out of critical condition, makes me feel as if a ton of the weight has been lifted off of my shoulders. The only thing to do now is catch the person who attacked her before they try to finish the job or worse, attack someone else."

"What makes you think that they will try to finish the job or go after someone else," Jose asked as he sat down next to Jason on the curb.

"They tried to frame me for the murder of Jessica. If they find out she's alive they will be forced to finish the job. The way she was attacked was from the front, so she saw her attacker. If they don't find out that she is alive then they might attack someone else in order to get me out of hiding. No matter what, we need to solve this case soon because the longer we wait the more we can potentially lose."

"Sir, are you ready to go," Dean asked as he pulled up in front of Jason and Jose.

"If you don't mind can you drop me off in little Italy," Jason asked as he got in the car.

"No problem sir, do you want me to drop off Mr. Rogers."

"I think it's best to keep Jose with us. His apartment is not safe so I rather have him stay with me, where I know it's safe. The only thing is, the place we are heading to right now is the opposite of safe," Jason said as he fiddled with the radio.

"Jason, the least I can do is help out in any way possible. If we have to go to another shady bar, then you can count me in," Jose chimed in from the back seat.

"I think you should stay in the car rather than join me. The person I am going to meet is not the friendliest and will certainly not be happy to see me."

"Are you meeting an ex-lover, sir," Dean asked as he made a left onto the Manhattan Bridge.

"Ex-lover, I wish. I'm about to walk into the lion's den, a restaurant named Gio's. The owner of the restaurant is the notorious mobster Max DeLuca. Since I put some of his guys away, he might want to get even," Jason said with a serious look on his face.

"When I think that things can't get any more dangerous, you have to go and prove me wrong. Can't we ever talk to a normal witness like an old lady," Jose whined.

"You make me laugh Jose, two seconds ago you were ready to go and now you're scared. I might not walk out of that restaurant in one piece. The only reason that I am going to see Max is to confirm a theory I have. So no matter how bad things might turn, I have to face them head on."

"What theory is that sir, if you don't mind sharing," Dean asked

"My theory is pretty simple; if the mafia was involved they would have just gone after me. They would have broken my kneecap or hand, but they never go after women or children. "

"So why would you want to see them, if you already know that they had nothing to do with Jessica," Jose asked as he tried to understand Jason's thought process.

"They might not be involved in this crime, but they might know someone who attacks victims the way Jessica was attacked. I know it's a stretch, but I need as many clues as I can get. Jose, you are not a detective, you just happened to be at the wrong place at the wrong time. There is no reason for you to get mixed up with the mafia on my behalf."

"Don't worry Jason; I'm doing this for myself. All of my life I have been told that I will never amount to anything. I dropped out of school to chase my passion, photography. That same passion has led me to you, even though it is under these horrific circumstances. I don't know anything about you but I believe in fate. So no matter what happens, I will see this through the end with you," Jose slammed his hands onto his thighs making a loud clapping sound.

"You have a change of heart every fifteen minutes, when this case is done I want to have you tested for bipolar disorder. If you do come with me inside the restaurant then you must follow my words exactly"

The sound of gulping resonated throughout the car. Both Jose and Dean were as quiet as church mice. The full severity of dealing with the Italian Mafia had finally sunk in. One false move could cost the group their lives.

"Jason, I will follow you to find Jessica's attacker, so please give me guidance."

"I applaud your courage and I will do whatever is in my power to make sure that you survive this meeting. The key thing you must remember is respect, never disrespect them. I remember my first time dealing with them; Ryan disrespected one of them by making a crude joke."

"Who's Ryan and what did they do to him," Jose asked.

"Wow, they really don't mention his name in the media. Ryan is my partner and that day he learned to never disrespect a member of the mob. When we walked outside, his car was in such bad condition that calling it a wreck would have been a compliment."

"If you have a partner how come he isn't helping out with this case? Wouldn't it be better to have all hands on deck?"

"I thought of calling him in to help many times but I don't want to see him get hurt. Whenever there is a chase or an important decision, he tends to freeze up and not follow through. Since this case is dangerous, it's best that he stays out of harm's way."

"Sir, we have arrived at the restaurant," Dean commented as he pulled into an empty parking space.

"Dean, park the car and just wait for us to come out," Dean nodded his head. "Jose are sure you want to do this," without any hesitation, Jose opened his car door and walked towards the restaurant. "I guess that's a yes," Jason said as he exited the car.

As the two of them tried to walk inside of the restaurant they were greeted by a tall gentleman in all black, "Can I help you with something? Gio's is booked for the night; I suggest you dine at another establishment."

"You know that would be a good idea, except I think my name is on the guest list. Max DeLuca is a very close friend and he always told me to stop by if I was ever in the neighborhood. Can you do me a favor and tell him that Jason Streak is here to take him up on his offer," Jason said while looking up to the bouncer.

The bouncer knocked on the door and another huge gentleman poked his head through the door. After a brief interaction, the bouncer went inside and the second one stood watch outside. After about five minutes the first bouncer came back.

"You are allowed to come in under one condition," the bouncer said to Jason.

"What's the condition, do I have to pay a cover charge?"

"The condition is this," the bouncer said and without warning he punched Jason in the gut.

Jason's knees buckled and he felt some of his stitches open up. Before he knew it, Jason was looking at the pavement, his body was arched over. He heard Jose's voice but the pain was the focus of his attention. When he looked in Jose's direction, he saw a look of concern on his face. Jason lifted his hand and showed Jose a thumbs up to signify that he was okay, "So can we go in now," he asked as he stood up.

"Let me show you in,' the bouncer said as he opened the door and allowed them to enter. All of the tables in the restaurant were empty except for three tables in the middle that had been joined together. The bouncer led the duo to the table and left.

The joined tables were filled with around twenty people all dressed in fine suits. They were in the middle of a nice meal and they were upset because more than half of their food remained on their plates. At the middle of the table, there sat a man in his mid-thirties who was considered untouchable by the NYPD, Max DeLuca.

"Jason Streak, to what do I owe this pleasure," DeLuca said as he rose from his seat. Everyone who had their backs to Jason had now turned to face him. DeLuca walked around the table and stopped in front of Jose, "Don't tell me this is your muscle, you came here with this? Your last partner looked like he could fight, this guy looks like a little lamb. So Mary tell me why you are here."

"I see that you and your buddies are celebrating my demise. I am the prime suspect in an ongoing investigation, that's fine but tomorrow I'm a free man."

"Why in the world would I celebrate your demise? You know as well as I do, if you really wanted to commit a crime no one would ever find out. Today's celebration is for my dear cousin little Frankie. Due to evidence tampering, he was acquitted of all his charges. So are you here to apologize to Frankie and everything you put him through? You had him arrested in front his family, just so you could try to crack him and get to me. Well here's your chance!"

"Frankie, I'm sorry about what happened to you. I followed the evidence and I had absolutely no knowledge of it being tampered with. Mr. DeLuca I also want to apologize to you, for giving you a bad impression of private investigators," Jason bowed his head in the direction of Frankie and DeLuca.

"What's with the formalities, Mr. Deluca forget about it. Call me Max," Deluca placed his hand on Jason's shoulder, "I'm just breaking your balls kid and you're a straight shooter. I like you because you have respect and rest assured none of my associates had anything to do with this matter. If you and I were to ever do battle, it would be of the mind, I would love to play against you in a game of chess and see how your mind really works."

"Thanks, Max.do you know anyone who attacks a person the way Jessica was attacked?"

"No, I never heard of anyone who attacks victims in that way. What I can tell you is that someone was looking for a yegg. They wanted them for a rush job and they were paying big."

"This is a big clue, thanks. A safe cracker would explain how they broke into the house. I think its best that I head on out before your dinner gets cold."

"That sounds like a good idea, let me walk you guys to the door," Max said as he pointed to the door.

As soon as they arrived at the exit, Jason turned to Jose, "Jose, I'll meet you outside in a bit I just have to ask Max one last question," After Jose was through the doors he turned to face Max, "By chance do you happen to know where I can purchase some oxycodone."

"What that little love tap from Lorenzo was too much for you to handle," Max jokingly asked.

"You should have him take boxing lessons because he hits like a girl. He just managed to scratch my stitches and they reopened. I need a sub and a half worth," Jason pulled out a hundred and fifty dollars from his wallet.

Max grabbed the money from Jason's hand, "Give me a couple of minutes," he then disappeared into the back. After a couple of minutes, he came out holding a small container, "You have six pills in here, don't take more than two pills within an eight hour period. These are really strong, trust me."

"It's been a pleasure doing business with you, Max," Jason grabbed the container and shook DeLuca's hand. Jason opened the door and walked out. The car was still parked across the street and Jose was already inside. As he walked to the car, he opened the container and took out two pills. By the time he entered the car, the pills were already dissolving in his stomach.

"Mr. Rogers was just telling me about your encounter with Mr. DeLuca. Don't you find it odd that he was so helpful? Also where to sir," Dean asked as he started the car.

"Many things were strange about the conversation, like his cousin Frankie. What evidence was tampered and who tampered the evidence," Jason said as he reclined his chair back, "DeLuca knows more than he's letting on, my gut is telling me he knows who is behind the attack. The key to solving this case is the safe cracker. I need to call Pavel in the morning to tell him about this lead. For now, we should all just rest up at the safe house."

"No problem sir, we should get there within the hour."

Jason nodded his head and closed his eyes. The pills were already taking effect, so he decided to relax. When he opened his eyes he was lying on the kitchen counter getting stitched up by Father Montgomery, "Hey, what's going on padre," Jason asked as he tried to sit up.

"Jason just stay still while I try to close your wound. Listen I know you're going through a lot right now but doing harm to your body is not the answer," Father Montgomery said as he closed the wound.

"Doing what harm to my body, I just drank too much on an empty stomach. You know what, just wake me up at eight tomorrow. It's going to be a big day," Jason closed his eyes and began to snore.

CHAPTER 9

The sound of applause filled the air; it was loud enough to wake Jason up. He got off of the table and walked towards the origin of the sound. He walked through the main hallway to find Father Montgomery and a couple of the nuns celebrating in the living room. They were all standing in front of the television.

"So who won the lottery," Jason asked as he approached the group.

"How can anyone here win the lottery, we do not gamble because that is a sin," one of the sister responded without turning around.

"It was a joke sister, so what's with all the celebrating?"

"You are no longer the suspect in the assault case. Apparently, they have a photograph of the real suspect. Look there it is on the television," Father Montgomery pointed at a picture on the screen.

The photo displayed on the screen showed Jason sleeping on the couch and a man walking on the roof. The next photo was a close-up of the suspect pointing at the camera. The photo had been enhanced to show the face, "The man in this picture has been identified as Moskey Kopylenko. He is armed and very dangerous if you have any information regarding his whereabouts please notify the proper authorities. Up next we have the best slice of pizza in the city. Stay tuned you don't…" Father Montgomery turned off the television.

"It seems that the evidence I brought the commissioner, was enough to clear my name. Where are Jose and Dean sleeping, I need to wake them up? Today is the day we catch ourselves a criminal."

"Jose is sleeping in your room and that fellow Dean left about an hour ago. He said he got called in to work. Go wake up Jose and bathe, in the meantime I will prepare breakfast for both of you," Father Montgomery said as he walked towards the kitchen.

"There's no need to cook anything for us, we can grab a bite to eat later."

"Jason after how you acted last night, I think you should eat before leaving."

"You know what, I will eat breakfast," Jason responded. He then grabbed his phone out of his pocket and dialed the commissioner's number. After a couple of rings, his call was answered.

"Commissioner Pavel here, how can I help you?"

"Good morning commissioner, how's life treating you?"

"I don't know how you do it, but every time we hit a dead end, you always find one crucial piece of evidence that brings us to a new path. I want you to meet me down at Jessica's house in an hour."

"Not a problem commissioner, but do me a favor and look into Kopylenko's finances. A source of mine told me that someone was looking to hire a safecracker for a rush job which paid well."

"I'll have someone look into it, see you soon."

Jason hung up the phone and knocked on the door in front of him.

"Come in Jason, I'm decent."

"Did my phone call wake you, Jose?" Jason asked as he opened the door and saw Jose sitting down on the bed.

"Couldn't sleep, I think yesterday was the most action packed day of my life. It feels as if my blood was replaced by adrenaline. Is this feeling normal when investigating a case?"

"Actually it is, after working on a case you feel like Superman. A prime example is when I chased after you even though I was still hurt from my last case. I'm going to go and take a shower but wait for me downstairs. Father Montgomery is making breakfast, so go eat we have a bigger day in front of us. Today we catch a criminal."

"No problem, boss."

"Hey, if you keep it up you might find yourself actually working for me," Jason walked out the room and headed towards the bathroom. After a quick shower, Jason was in the room changing out of the priest clothes. In less than twenty minutes, Jason was showered, changed and heading down for breakfast. Right before he opened the door to the kitchen, he popped a pain killer.

"I made you an omelet, so eat up," father Montgomery said while bringing Jason a plate of food.

"Thanks, but can I get it to go? I have to make it to the crime scene in the next forty minutes."

"I'll drive you down there, so bring the food with you and also bring a bottle of water."

"Father, you know I can just take a cab to the crime scene. There is no reason for you to drive all the way to Manhattan for me."

"Sister Christine confessed her sins to me last night. This is the least I can do especially after the way one of my nuns treated you. I'll go and bring the car around."

"So do you think that this guy, Moskey will lead us to the person who paid him," Jose asked as they walked outside.

"Moskey Kopylenko is what you would call a seasoned veteran. It's going to be hard to get a name out of him if we are lucky he might slip up and give us a new clue."

"How do you know that he won't sell out his employer," Jose asked as they entered the car.

"I've dealt with him many times in the past, however, he never once ratted out any of his associates. "

"So he just stays quiet while being interrogated?"

"I wish he stayed quiet, he loves to talk just not about the crime. I remember one time he spoke to a detective for an hour straight about a date he went on. The officer was forced to listen because it was his alibi regarding a jewelry store heist. He's cocky but smart; hopefully, the evidence will make him cooperate."

"What do you think are the odds of the police tracking down Mr. Kopylenko," Father Montgomery asked.

"Honestly, the chances of the police finding him are very low. I was able to evade the authorities and if I wanted to, I could have left the country. If I could hide, imagine a seasoned criminal," Jason said while handing his empty plate to Jose.

"So if we are unable to locate him, how are we supposed to solve this case," Jose blurted out as he grabbed the plate and sat it on the seat next to him.

"It is quite simple my dear Watson, we follow the money. We know someone paid him to break into

Jessica's house. We should be able to check his financials to find out who paid him."

"On all those crime shows, criminals get paid in cash. If he was paid in cash, would you be able to track it," Father Montgomery asked as he exited the FDR.

"It is true that most criminals get paid in cash. If he did get paid in cash then that lead is dead. Since it was a rush job, he may have been paid by wire transfer. Sometimes it is hard to come up with tens of thousands of dollars in cash. Liquidating large sums can raise a couple of red flags."

"Jason, how did you learn all of this, did you go to John Jay and study criminal justice," Jose leaned forward to hear Jason's response.

"I learned through personal experience and reading. This line of work requires a good understanding of the human psyche. So I make it my duty to read as many books as I can, just so I can stay one step ahead of the game."

"Wow don't you get bored from only reading books about human psychology? I always hated reading non-fiction because it gets boring."

"Don't worry I also read biographies and nonfiction. I just finished the book Retirement Bloodbath by Joshua Rodriguez, I couldn't put it down. I personally enjoy reading but Ryan; he almost never picks up a book."

"You and your partner Ryan seem to have nothing in common, how did the two of you end up as private investigators?"

"I always loved reading mystery novels, instead of playing cops and robbers growing up we played detective. His family was surprised when I received my private investigator license, I passed the test in one try and that's the short version of why I got into this line of work."

"What made Ryan join you?"

"You know, I have never asked him that. If I had to guess, I would say he joined just so he could spend time with me. While he was off in college, I worked alone only doing small cases. After he dropped out of college and joined me is when we started getting more cases. Ryan is great at marketing, without him I might still be working on missing pet cases."

"So you are the face of the company and he is the man behind the curtain? If he heard the news this morning, do you think he will also be at the crime scene?"

"That is a good question, Jose. I should call my office and tell him to meet me down there."

"Why wouldn't you call his cell phone directly?"

"Ryan has his phone set to automatic rejection for private callers and he rarely listens to his voicemails. The phone I am using is set to private and virtually untraceable, so it's easier for me to call my office. Also if he doesn't pick up then my receptionist will. Give me a minute let me call," Jason took the phone out of his pocket and dialed his office. After a couple of rings, his call was directed to the answering machine, "I guess Amanda is running late. This is Jason; I'm going down to Jessica's house to meet with the detectives. Meet me down there; I want to go over the clues. If you need to contact me just call Pavel," Jason hung up the phone.

"I think this is as far as I can take you," Father

Montgomery said as he stopped in front of Cardinal Avenue.

The entrance to Cardinal Avenue was blocked off by three squad cars and yellow police tape. Other than the three squad cars there were at least a dozen officers present along with an ambulance.

"Jose, let's go see what's going on. Father Montgomery thanks for the ride."

"Stay safe, Jason I mean it," Father Montgomery said as they left his car.

Jason and Jose had to walk through a small mob of people just to make it to the police tape. A couple of the people in the crowd realized who he was and started bombarding him with questions. Luckily one of the officers at the police line noticed Jason and he lifted the tape so that he could enter.

"Whoa there, can I help you with something," the officer said as he extended his arm out to stop Jose from passing the line.

"It's okay Carlos, he's with me," Jason said as he lifted the tape for Jose.

"Sorry about that Mr. Streak, I didn't know that he worked with you."

"No worries Carlos, how's the family?"

"They are fine, thanks for asking."

"What's going on here, why the police tape and squad cars? I spoke to the commissioner earlier about my arrival, is all this really necessary?"

"We actually found Moskey Kopylenko, that's why we have secured the perimeter."

"Does he have a hostage or something; I don't get the need of an ambulance. Am I able to speak with him?"

"If you want to speak you would need an

Ouija board."

"Moskey Kopylenko is dead," Jose shouted out. All of a sudden the crowd began to take photos and talk loudly.

"Jose, shush! Carlos, please elaborate."

"Certainly, he was found dead this morning inside of 1727 Cardinal Avenue."

CHAPTER 10

"Carlos, who is the detective in charge right now," Jason asked the officer.

"Right now Detective Morales is the lead investigator on the case. Do you want me to take you guys to him?"

"Can you?"

"Sure, let me just get someone to take over my position," the officer grabbed his walkie-talkie, "this is Officer Lopez, I have Jason Streak here with me. Can you send someone here to the line, so that I can bring him to Detective Morales?"

"I'll come up and get him myself," said a voice from the radio.

"Thanks for that Carlos."

"No problem sir."

Jason waited there with Jose and Carlos for about five minutes, before a stout man in jeans, approached the group, "Streak, how glad I am to have you back on our side," he shouted.

"But detective, I never left the side of justice. Like a prodigal son, I was cast out of the garden."

"Listen, Streak, I don't have time to argue about your weird analogies, so hurry up and follow me to the crime scene," Detective Morales said as he began walking back in the direction he came. Jason and Jose followed behind, "Moskey Kopylenko was found dead this morning approximately forty minutes ago. The cause of death was a single puncture wound to the chest. According to the medical examiner's preliminary report, the murder took place last night between the hours of eight and nine pm."

"Is the blade the same one that was used to attack Jessica Holmes?"

"We can't be a hundred percent certain but from the looks of it, the knife that committed this murder is the same one used in the attack on Ms. Holmes. Are you sure you want to see the body here in the house? You could look at it in the coroner's office back at the station," Detective Morales asked as he walked up the stair to Jessica's house.

"Why wouldn't I want to look at the body here?"

"After seeing those photos of you and her, I thought this would be the last place you would want to visit."

"It's alright Detective Morales; I know how to separate my personal life from my work life. The one you should be worried about is this one over here," Jason pointed at Jose, "This is his first crime scene and it actually might be his first time seeing a dead body."

"Listen here, you better not throw up on the corpse. Promise me you that you will not vomit on the body."

"I promise, Mr. Detective," Jose said in a cracking voice.

"It's Detective Morales," the detective snapped at Jose.

"Come on Jamie, be nice to the kid, he's new."

"Streak constantly finds a way to make a mockery of my crime scenes, now he's bringing interns to the scene of a murder. God help me if this kid vomits on the corpse," Detective Morales muttered under his breath, as he entered the house alone.

Before Jason could walk into the house, Jose stopped him, "Jason, will I really vomit after seeing the body? I don't want to you to get in trouble if I do happen to vomit."

"He's messing with you Jose; it's an old wives tale. Never in all my years of investigation, have I seen someone vomit at the sight of a dead body. Staring at a dead body has never hurt anyone. Let's hurry on inside before Detective Morales starts yelling at us."

They walked inside of Jessica's house; it was crawling with police personnel. The corpse was hard to miss, it was on the couch. The killer had positioned the body in the exact way that Jason's body was when he slept there the night of the attack. Before inspecting the body thoroughly, Jason grabbed a pair of latex gloves for himself and Jose.

"Here put these on, we can't have you disturbing evidence," he said as he handed Jose one of the pairs of gloves. Jason proceeded to inspect the corpse.

Once Jose had the gloves on, he joined Jason at the corpse, "Jason, I think I'm going to wait outside."

"Are you sure Jose, because I think this could be a valuable experience for you," Jason said as he turned around to face Jose. "You don't look so good, are you alright Jose?"

Before Jose could respond, he turned his back away from Jason and started vomiting on the living room floor. Immediately everyone in the room was staring at Jose. After Jose was finished vomiting, a sudden silence filled the room. It didn't last long since it was broken by a shout.

"I TOLD YOU THIS WAS GOING TO HAPPEN!" Detective Morales shouted as he reentered the living room. "Can someone clean this mess up, before I lose it?"

"Technically you told him not to vomit on the corpse. As we can all see plain as day, he did not vomit on the corpse. In his defense, he did eat breakfast not too long ago. Also, nobody warned us that there was a rotting corpse on the couch before we ate," Jason jokingly said, as he tried to ease the tension in the room.

"Streak, you are lucky that the commissioner likes you. If it were up to me you would be behind bars right now, just look at how the killer left the body. Sure looks a lot like you in that photo."

"I don't get you, detective, one second you are concerned about me and the next you have a vendetta against me," Jason said as he walked to Detective Morales.

Detective Morales got even closer until their faces were mere inches apart, "Streak I was never concerned about you. I just acted nicely to see if you would let your guard down. You go to from the most wanted man in New York to ally of the police within the span of a couple of days. Then you come to an active crime scene and destroy crucial evidence. Anyone with a shred of common sense can tell something is fishy about you and your story."

"What crucial evidence was destroyed? Are you accusing me of killing Moskey Kopylenko? Is that what you are trying to do detective? If it is, then just come out and say it to me. Do you want to know where I was last night between the hours of eight and nine pm last night?"

"Yes, I am accusing you of this murder. Where were you last night between the hours of eight and nine pm? Please tell me you were out with his highness, the Duke of Puke. If that happens to be your alibi, then you are better off confessing right now."

"I was at a dinner between the hours of eight and nine pm. How about you, where were you during those hours?"

"You think this is a game, I'm the one asking the questions here! Who is your witness so that I can send one of these uniforms to verify your story?"

"The dinner was at Gio's, and there were about twenty people other than Jose who can vouch for me. Just ask Max DeLuca, he was the one who invited me. You see it was a party for his little cousin Frankie. I'm sure you want to verify my alibi yourself, so enjoy."

"Why am I not surprised that you surround yourself with scum like DeLuca? Who's to say that you didn't hire him to take care of Kopylenko? Keep on digging a deeper hole for you; I love to watch my prey squirm."

"That's enough! Both of you stand down and separate this instant," Commissioner Pavel's voice resonated throughout the brownstone.

"Look at that, the master comes to save his pet once again," Detective Morales said as he stomped out of the building.

"Back for less than an hour and you are already making a scene. Please tell me that you are actually here to work rather than here to argue with Morales."

"Commissioner, I already found some weird

things about Kopylenko's body. I was about to take a closer look at it. Another set of trained eye would be pretty helpful that is if you don't mind."

"Sure, let me take a look," Commissioner Pavel stopped and looked down at the ground. "Did I just step in vomit? I'm not even going to ask how this got here, but I want it cleaned. Clinton, clean this mess up!

"Let's get back to Kopylenko's body, take a look at his hands."

"What about them, they are broken? He was probably tortured before his death."

"That's what the killer wanted us to think. Who would torture someone and only stab them once? If you are torturing someone, you would drag their death for as long as possible."

"Jason, why would the killer make it look like they had tortured the body?"

"It's simple commissioner, the killer wanted to mislead us. They wanted us to think this murder was mafia hit."

"A mafia hit? Jason, broken hands don't scream out mafia hit. He was a safe cracker so it looks like someone tortured him by taking away his craft."

"That's not what makes this look like a mafia hit, this is," Jason said as he opened Kopylenko's mouth. He stuck his hand inside the mouth and pulled out a small black object.

"Is that a rat? How did you know there was something in there," Jose asked as he began gagging.

"It's an old tradition of the mob when they kill a snitch; they stick a rat in their mouth. It's done to show that the person was in their eyes a rat. Were you the one who vomited on the floor?"

"Sorry about that commissioner, the smell was just so bad."

"Don't worry about it son, you just owe me a new pair of shoes. Jason your intern poses a good question, how did you know that was there?"

"I actually didn't know it was a rat, but I knew something was stuffed in his mouth. From seeing Mr. Kopylenko on multiple occasions, I noticed that his cheeks were a bit puffier than I remembered. Other than the rat in his mouth, he is also missing his tongue."

"From everything you've told me, this seems to be a mob hit. What makes you think that it's not a mob hit?"

"I met with DeLuca last night; he was celebrating the release of his cousin Frankie. All of his captains were there along with his enforcers. He's the one who told me that someone was looking to hire a safecracker for a rush job. Why would he tell me to look into a safe cracker if he was having him killed while we spoke?"

"Max DeLuca loves psychological warfare. He probably told you that to throw you off his scent. It seems to me that Kopylenko was hired to frame you for the murder of Ms. Holmes, then when he found out she was alive he wanted to come clean. DeLuca couldn't let that happen so he had him killed. He coincidently was at a party with a bunch of his men and then the man he tried to frame stopped by. What do you think of my deduction Jason?"

"It's a pretty good theory too bad that it is just a theory and not what actually occurred."

"What makes think I am wrong about this?

Don't tell me that the mob doesn't go after women or children, times have changed. I need solid evidence, so tell me do you have evidence to disprove my theory?"

"The body commissioner is my evidence. The only ones who knew how I slept on that couch are Jessica's attackers. Kopylenko was not alone when he broke into Jessica's apartment."

"Jason that picture of you sleeping on the couch has been circulating the news since five this morning."

"Exactly commissioner five am, Kopylenko was killed between the hours of eight and nine pm. The person who hired him is Jessica's attacker and also a murderer. In all of our dealings with Kopylenko, he never once sold out any of his accomplices. The only reason he would come back to the scene is to speak with his employer. So commissioner why would Kopylenko request to meet with his employer? Especially after the job was completed?"

"Maybe he wanted the rest of his payment?"

"Kopylenko was a professional, one of the best he always knew how to receive payment. My theory is that he received his entire payment in full, except the funds never fully cleared. So he was not paid in cash so if we check his financial records. We will eventually find his employer."

"Wow Streak, you are absolutely right. His financial records actually do tell us a lot," Detective Morales said as he entered the living room carrying a stack of papers.

"See commissioner, the finances were the missing piece. What do the finances tell us, detective?"

"The finances tell us that you are under arrest Jason Streak. You have the right to remain silent. Anything you say can and will be used against you in a court of law. You have the right to an attorney. If you cannot afford an attorney, one will be provided for you. Do you understand the rights I have just read to you?"

"Are you serious, detective?"

"As serious as a heart attack, let's take a ride downtown Streak."

CHAPTER 11

"What's your reason for arresting Jason, Morales," Pavel asked.

"Streak said it himself; Kopylenko's payment was traced back to Streak's own agency. So Streak, do you care to explain why your agency paid Mr. Kopylenko eight thousand dollars?"

"That makes no sense, was he paid by check or wire transfer," Jason asked as he backed away from Detective Morales.

"I don't see why the payment method matters. Stop asking questions and start answering my questions."

"Morales, just answer Jason's questions. Please explain how you were able to trace the payment back to Jason's agency," Pavel asked as he stepped in front of Jason.

"Kopylenko was paid through a wire transfer from a shell corporation. The shell company was formed a couple of months ago. Prior to the date of the assault, the account only had a hundred dollars in it. The shell company was wired the funds at five pm. From there the funds were transferred to Mr. Kopylenko's account at seven pm. After we froze Streak's finances, the transfer was recalled."

"Unfortunately Morales, you are accusing an innocent man. There is no way that he was able to transfer funds at five pm because he was at a pub with me. We were drinking during happy hour and he did not have a laptop or tablet with him. The whole time we were drinking he never took out his phone. If you want a sober witness, then I can call the bartender down to the station."

"Jason was at the mall at the time the funds were transferred to Mr. Kopylenko's account," Jose blurted out.

"The Duke decides to speak. Tell me, Duke, what proof do you have that he was at the mall?"

"If you want proof ask anyone who was in the mall that day. I chased Jose up and down that mall; I think there might even be a viral video of the chase online. Also please call him Jose and not Duke," Jason said as he emerged from behind the commissioner.

"Jason other than yourself, who else had access to your agency's finances," Pavel asked as he turned to face Jason.

"There's only three other people who have access to the agency's bank account. The people who have access to that account are Neil my accountant, Amanda my secretary and of course Ryan."

"Morales put out an APB on Amanda and Ryan. Also send out some uniforms to their place of residence. I want both of them found, remember one of them is a killer."

"Commissioner, both Ryan, and Amanda should be at the office working. Why are you only putting an APB out on Ryan and Amanda?"

"I stopped by the office before arriving here and all the lights were off. Also last night I emailed both Amanda and Ryan the photos from the memory card. I can't believe it myself that one of them might be a murderer."

"Just because you emailed the photos to them, doesn't make one of them a murderer. Someone could have forced them to transfer that money out of the account. Remember that even though you sent the photos it was sent after Kopylenko was murdered."

"Jason, I know this may be hard for you to understand but someone close to you is behind this. Think about all the murders you have solved over the years, how many of them were committed by someone close to the victim?"

"About fifty percent of the murders were committed by someone close to the victim. I wasn't the victim Jessica was and then Moskey. How can it...."

"Stop focusing on the dot Streak," Detective Morales cut Jason off mid-sentence. "The attacker used both Ms. Holmes and Mr. Kopylenko to frame you. Why else would an anonymous tip be called in about Ms. Holmes' attack? The attacker would have succeeded in framing you except you woke up and left the house."

"It's scary but for the first time, Morales is on your side, Jason. I want an officer with you at all times. No investigating on your own, this is a direct order Jason," said Pavel sternly.

"Okay, I will have an officer with me at all times. I need to go to my office and collect some things. Can I borrow Officer Lopez for my journey?"

"Streak, didn't you hear the commissioner? Your safety is one of our top priorities, you can't keep on playing detective," Detective Morales shouted at Jason.

"Jason is going to your office worth risking your life," Pavel asked.

Jason took a second to answer, "Yes commissioner this trip to my office is worth my life. I need my work laptop; it will be able to tell me who transferred the funds out of my account. I will also be picking up my Walther P38 to aide in my defenses."

"I will allow it as long as you do not leave Officer Lopez' side."

"I promise that I will have Carlos with me the whole time. You will not regret this sir."

"Officer Lopez, come to the crime scene immediately," Detective Morales yelled into a nearby officer's walkie-talkie.

In a matter of minutes, Officer Lopez arrived out of breath, "Officer Lopez reporting in."

"Lopez, I want you to take Streak to his office. You are not to leave his side at any point if he wants to use the restroom you shall accompany him. Do you understand?"

"Yes, I understand sir. Am I only to bring Mr. Streak to his office or his associate as well?"

"Let me bring Jose with us. He will stay in the car while we go upstairs, I promise," Jason pleaded to the commissioner."

"It's your call, Morales," Pavel responded.

"Well, I don't want any more vomit here so take him with you. Keep him in the car; I don't want him screwing anything up."

"You heard the Detective let's get going Jose," Jason said as he hobbled out the house. His painkiller was losing its effect so he took another. He looked at the bottle and saw that there were two left.

"Follow me," Carlos said as he led Jason and Jose to a patrol car that was parked a block away from Jessica's house. The trio got in the car and drove towards Jason's office.

"Jose, when we get to the office I want you to stay in the car."

"I don't know why I can help. It's not like the killer is in your office waiting for you."

"You will be more helpful in the car Jose. Not even I can predict what's going to happen inside of my office. That's why I need you to stay in the car because you can call for backup. Going upstairs should only take at most ten minutes. If we aren't back in ten minutes use the radio to call for backup."

"What if I call for reinforcements and you guys walk out moments later?"

"If that happens then we will handle it. The most important thing is for you to make that call."

"You ready to go inside, Jason," Carlos asked as he parked the patrol car in front of a fire hydrant.

"I'm ready, Jose come sit up front," Jason said as he opened the back door for him. "Keep the doors locked at all times."

"Jason, just make sure that you come back in one piece. Remember Jessica needs to see you when she wakes up."

"Don't worry, I'll make sure he stays safe," Carlos said right before he and Jason entered the skyscraper.

"Press twenty for me Carlos," Jason said to Carlos as he entered the elevator.

"The twentieth floor, why so high up. What if the elevator breaks down, do you expect your clients to walk all the way up?"

"Not my idea to get an office in the sky. Heck if the elevator stops working I'm not even coming into work. The rent is double what we paid in Staten Island but the view is nice. After you Officer Lopez," Jason said as the elevator doors opened.

"I think this is the first time you have called

me Officer Lopez. Man does it sound weird to hear you say it. Come here and open the door, it's locked."

Jason took out his keys and unlocked the door of the detective agency, as he pushed the door open the sound of nails to a chalkboard filled the corridor.

"Is that your door?"

"Yup, it works better than having a bell on the door."

"Who is that lying on the floor bleeding," Carlos asked as he rushed over to inspect the person on the ground.

Jason rushed over, "Dean what are you doing here and why is there a gun in your hand!?"

"Turn around sir," Dean said in a soft tone.

The lights in the office suddenly came on. Carlos immediately grabbed his gun and turned around.

"Pol…." before he could say the word police, Carlos' body went limp.

The sounds of nails to a chalkboard filled the room as the door was closed. Jason looked up from Carlos' dead body. His eyes were met by a suppressor on the barrel of a Beretta M9.

"So you're the one behind all of this!!!"

CHAPTER 12

"Don't tell me that the great Jason Streak didn't see this coming. Don't you pride yourself on being able to calculate the outcome of any situation? Well, tell me, Jason did you see this coming?"

"Nope, you actually managed to surprise me. Who would think that you would shoot my cab driver friend," Jason answered sarcastically.

"You think you're funny, I can see right through you. You're losing your mind right now aren't you?"

"I'm not the one who is going around shooting cab drivers and killing police officers. You, my dear friend, are losing your mind. Why did you do it, Ryan?"

"Are you kidding me, you honestly don't know why? First of all, I did not shoot a cab driver, I shot an FBI agent."

"Ryan are you on drugs, that's Dean my cab driver. Talk to me buddy, what's going on up there?"

"Jason you are so oblivious to everything. What cab driver has an FBI badge and a gun? Your friend Dean was investigating our agency. I did it all for us and yet you got all the credit"

"Why would the FBI investigate us and what do you mean you did it all for us. What credit? Can you form a proper sentence?"

"I tampered with evidence, Jason. How else do you think we solved most of those impossible cases?"

"Ryan, did you fake evidence just so that we could arrest Frankie DeLuca?"

"Yes, Jason, you dimwit I faked the evidence that put him in jail. That's probably why the FBI is investigating us."

"Why would you do that, we could have put him away using real evidence. Do you not realize how illegal and unjust that is? So other than shooting an FBI operative, killing a cop, killing a criminal, attacking Jessica and framing me you also tampered with evidence."

"Yup, that pretty much sums up everything. I did all of that for us and yet I was never recognized."

"Ryan I've known you all of my life, this isn't like you. Ryan, who doesn't recognize you, talk to me, bro."

"You know me, Jason all you care about is yourself. You had to move in and ruin everything. You always were top of the class, if I got a hundred on a test you somehow managed to get a hundred and five. I went to college out of state just so I didn't have to deal with you. I was so happy when you told me that you weren't going to college. You wanted to become a private investigator, I laughed. I thought for sure you would fail but of course, Jason Streak never fails. My parents raved about how successful you were at solving little cases and how I should be more like you. So I did what any good son would, I quit school and joined you. Guess what, my parents still only spoke about your achievements."

"Ryan, what does this have to do with any of the people you hurt? You were a little jealous; do you want me to apologize for getting better grades than you?"

"You still don't see it, do you? You have been on multiple interviews on television, while I have to sit in the crowd. I wasn't even allowed in the green room. Do you know how many times my name was mentioned in the paper? Once and they called me 'Brian the sidekick'. No one ever mentions the stuff I do on these cases."

"Ryan, I thank you all the time for your help."

"You think just saying thank you is enough? You get special treatment wherever you go. No one has ever heard of Ryan Barnes. See everything would be fine if she didn't come to the office."

"Are you talking about Jessica? What does she have to with your mental breakdown?"

"She was the last straw. She came into the office and you already marked her as yours."

"You were against us taking the case. How was I supposed to know that you wanted to talk to her? You never showed any interest in her."

"It's called playing hard to get. You messed up everything, you're the reason that no one even knows I exist," Ryan screamed as he put the tip of the barrel on Jason's forehead.

"You're wrong Ryan, I'm not to blame. Whenever it's your turn to bat you freeze up before you take the first swing. Do you want to know why I had to jump through two panes of glass? I did it because you couldn't stop the criminal. The reason no one knows who you are is because you have never asserted yourself. I was happy when you decided to go to college because you had dreams. The Ryan from back then had some drive, he wasn't afraid of failing. You let other people's opinion affect you."

"Do you think the world will know my name now!?"

"Actually yes, even though you acting like a

crazy man you are living for yourself. If you are going to shoot me then let me take some painkillers."

"Why?"

"It's because you don't know the pain I go through to make sure things get done. I bruised my ribs last week in that robbery case in queens. The doctor told me to rest for a week but I had to keep on working cases to pay the bills. Then I jumped through those glass panes and had to get stitches. The next day I ran into a cart in the mall while trying to catch a stalker, my stitches reopened. That same night I jumped off the roof of a brownstone and had to run for over a mile. Let me not forget to mention taking a blow to my gut from one of DeLuca's lackeys. I've been popping painkillers like they are candy. Not only am I in pain but I'm also stressed out. You wanted to have an office in the city; the rent is double what we were paying in Staten Island. So for us to keep up with the bills, I have to continue to work no matter what. Yet you don't see me going on a killing spree because of stress," Jason said as swallowed the last two of his pills.

"You're killing yourself by taking those pills; Mr. Perfect is a pill popper."

"So what I'm taking pills, I am not perfect. I would never claim to be perfect, I am human. The secret to my success is hard work; I don't know why you have me on a pedestal. You need to actually finish what you started."

"What are you talking about? Do you want me to shoot you?"

"I want you to actually finish something that you start. When we were kids and played detective you would always get mad and stop playing. You started college and as soon as it got hard you dropped out. Then you attacked Jessica and you couldn't even finish that. Her wound was shallow; she's going to make it. So no matter how you play with our corpses, she's going to name you as her attacker. You are now left with one of two options: Your first option is to drop your gun and surrender. Your second option is to kill both Dean and I. Both options lead to a one-way ticket to jail. Any second now the police will be here, so you better think fast."

"These are the last words I will ever hear from Jason Streak. Your ideology, that all outcomes can be calculated is false. You see the world as black and white, you never notice the grays. I see myself as your older brother and it is my duty to protect you at all costs. I did all this to teach you. You need to be able to see the grays, Jason you are growing up yet you know so little. You really think that I couldn't finish Jessica off? I attacked her, just to show you that you can't protect everyone. I didn't want to kill my little brother's girlfriend. I saw how she looked at you in the living room, I was there watching you, making sure she didn't hurt you. If you keep on living life recklessly, you will end up losing her. Your father died in a car accident because of you. He drove in that blizzard and into a tree because you were in the hospital. You caught pneumonia because you were out looking for a lost cat. I want you to learn that there are consequences in life."

"Police open up!!!"

"I guess our little chat is over, it's time for me face the consequences," Ryan said as he removed the suppressor off of his gun, "This is going to be the second time today that I proved that you can never expect the unexpected. I choose option three," Ryan said as he lifted the gun to his own head and pulled the trigger.

The sound of the gun was deafening, but it was followed shortly by the sound of the door getting kicked in. As the police rushed in, Jason's sight began to darken. The last thing Jason saw was the face of Officer Lopez lying next to him, then darkness.

CHAPTER 13

When Jason opened up his eyes, he saw that he was in a hospital bed. He looked around and saw Jose sleeping in one of the chairs, "Jose, sleeping on the job already?"

"Jason is that you," Jose asked as he woke up.

"No, it's the pillow talking to you. Of course, it's me, can you help me out of this bed"

"Sure, but Jason are you sure you should be walking? They did pump those pills out of your system," Jose said as he walked over and helped Jason out of the bed.

"Don't worry I'll be fine. So, how long have I been out for?"

"It's been two days since the incident. Officer Lopez' funeral took place this morning."

"Do you have a copy of yesterday's newspaper," Jason asked as he put on his jeans.

"Commissioner Pavel left a copy of yesterday's newspaper here. He also told me to tell you that you're welcome."

Jason removed his hospital gown and picked up the paper, "Last night, Police cornered suspect Ryan Barnes in the Private Eye detective agency. Barnes confessed to the framing of private investigator Jason Streak. Other than the attack on Ms. Holmes, Barnes is responsible for the death of a local locksmith and Officer Carlos Lopez. Barnes may have suffered from mental illnesses. After coming to the realization of his crimes, Barnes committed suicide. Agent Roberts of the FBI who assisted in this investigation had this to say: 'Our hearts go out to the families of the victims. Barnes was obsessed with Jason Streak and he let that obsession control his actions. If anyone out there is having similar feelings please seek help.' Jason Streak could not be reached for his thought on the matter," Jason put the paper down on the bed; "Jose is Jessica staying in this hospital?"

"Yeah, she's staying upstairs in room 523. She regained consciousness last night."

"Have you visited her Jose," Jason asked as he put on his sneakers.

"No, I can't visit her, I was stalking her. How would I even introduce myself? 'How are you Jessica, I'm Jose. I'm a photographer and I'm actually your stalker.' She'll probably have me arrested!"

"Jose you saved my life last night. You did as you were told and you rallied the cavalry. Let me help you fix things with Jessica," Jason said as he opened the door to his room and walked out.

Jose scurried to catch up to Jason, who was already out the room, "Don't you think you should wear a shirt? What if she wants me arrested?"

"That shirt has Carlos and Ryan's blood on it, so I'm not wearing it. She's not going to have you arrested. She's probably going to kick me out and say that she never wants to see me again," Jason said with a laugh as they walked into the elevator.

"Why wouldn't she want to see you, I don't get it."

"Like I told you before, she almost died because of me. There's no way that she will forgive me. I just want to say my peace and also make sure she doesn't press charges on you," Jason said as they walked out of the elevator.

"Do you want to buy some flowers from downstairs?"

"It's too late for that because we are already here," Jason said as he knocked on Jessica's door.

"Come in," said a familiar voice.

Jason opened the door and saw Dean standing over Jessica's bed. Dean was wearing a tailored suit with his right arm in a sling, "Hey," Jason said as he and Jose entered the room.

"Ms. Holmes, I think that you have answered enough questions for today. Jose, why don't you and I take a stroll?"

"Dean, that sounds like an amazing idea," Jose said as he walked right out the room.

"Good luck sir," Dean whispered to Jason. Dean walked out the room closing the door behind him.

Jason sat down in a chair next to Jessica's bed. He looked at her but was at a loss for words.

"So is Jose your new psychotic partner," Jessica asked.

"Actually he's your stalker," Jason jokingly said.

"So I got stabbed and hospitalized because of you and now you brought my stalker to meet me," Jessica said as she sat up in the bed.

"I'm sorry that you got injured because of me. I had no idea the Ryan was that messed up in the head; he even killed an officer friend of ours. He went out of control and hurt a lot of people and I can't help but feel like I caused all of this. I know that there is nothing I can do to fix what he did to you. I brought Jose here so that you could decide his fate. He saved my life the other day. He messed up but he's willing to take full responsibilities for his actions."

Jessica just sat there quietly.

"That's all I wanted to say. I'll understand if you never want to see me or Jose again," Jason said as he stood up from his chair and began walking away.

"Your friend Agent Roberts told me everything that happened. Is all of it true," Jessica asked.

Jason turned back and sat down on her bed, "That depends on what he told you."

"Is it true that you worked relentlessly to find my attacker? You even went as far as confronting the mob to get clues. He told me that one of those mobsters punched you in the street. Agent Roberts also told me how you saved his life by stalling Ryan."

"I did whatever I could to bring your attacker to justice. At the end of the case, Ryan killed himself. I failed at getting you your justice and I failed at saving my partner. It might not look like it but I'm in bad shape. I might even lose my private investigator license."

"Don't worry you look like crap," Jessica jokingly said.

Jason began to laugh, "Listen, I want to see how you look after you had your stomach pumped. I was actually thinking about getting a cup of coffee down at the cafeteria, do you want to join me?"

"I'll join you, let me get changed first."

"No problem, I'll wait."

"Jason, which means get out," she shouted at him.

"Jessica, I'll be outside," Jason said as he walked out the room.

"I can't believe you were right. She really doesn't want to see you anymore," Jose said to Jason.

"What are you talking about Jose? She kicked me out her room because she's changing her clothes. Also, why are the two of you sitting on the floor?"

"Sir, we were trying to listen in on your conversation," Dean said.

"Dean, I don't even know what I'm supposed to call you."

"Dean is still fine, sir."

"Thanks for lying to the media like that for me. This scandal could have buried my agency."

"The bureau would rather cover this up than let the truth come out. Who knows how many times he tampered with evidence."

"Are you ready to go, Jason," Jessica said as she stepped out into the hallway.

"I'm always ready Jessica. Jose, you better rest up because we have a lot of work to do tomorrow. Be at the office tomorrow by nine and make sure you bring your own laptop."

"He works for you now," Jessica asked him.

"Yeah, what she said," Jose said as he stood up.

"You said you were a freelancer and you even called me boss. So I figured you wanted a job. After all the strings I pulled to get you this job, you better show."

"What strings did you pull; you're the owner of the company."

"Sorry, I can't hear you. I think the gunshot the other day messed up my hearing. I'll talk to you later, I have a lunch date with this beautiful woman," Jason said as he and Jessica walked into the elevator.

"Who said this is a date," Jessica asked once they were alone in the elevator.

"I just thought you know because of the thing."

"It's still fun to mess with you," Jessica said as they walked out of the elevator and into the light.